Unraveled

Lori Bell

Cover photograph by Lori Bell

About.com Staging Myeloma, Sources: Kyle, Robert and Rajkumar, S. Vincent "Multiple Myeloma" *Blood* 15 March 2008 111:2962-2972; Lin, Pei "Plasma Cell Myeloma" *Hematology/ Oncology Clinics of North America* 2009 23:709-727; Nau, Konrad and Lewis, William "Multiple Myeloma: Diagnosis and Treatment" *American Family Physician* 1 October 2008 78:853-859.

Mayoclinic.org Aortic valve stenosis; williams-syndrome.org; litigationandtrial.com/2011/12/articles/attorney/medical-malpractice-1/anesthesia-malpractice/

Printed by CreateSpace

ISBN 978-1499540369

DEDICATION

To my husband, Mike for being the one for me, and to my children, Bailey and Connor for completing me. I love all three of you with all of my heart.

Chapter 1

The front door of her brick tricolor white, gray and black two-story house slams and Kelsey Walker hears her seventeen-year-old daughter, Bailey call out to her. When she walks into the living room, Bailey isn't alone.

"Mom, there is someone I'd like you to meet." Kelsey smiled at the young black teenage boy standing just a few inches taller than her daughter. He is wearing nice jeans that actually fit his body – unlike so many of the teenagers who now wear their pants below their waistline – and a pinstriped white dress shirt, neatly tucked in, minus a belt. She said *hello* and extended her hand when Bailey introduced her friend as "*Charlie.*"

"It's nice to meet you, Mrs. Newman," Charlie started to say, and then Bailey corrected him, "It's Walker. My mom is newly married." Kelsey laughed, and wanted to know more about Bailey's friend. She rarely ever brought a new friend home, and never a boy unless there were a group of boys and girls all together.

"So Charlie, you're a junior at Bond High School too?"

"Yes ma'am," he answered, "and Bailey and I have more than half of our classes together this year." Kelsey knew that meant Charlie, too, is an honors student.

"Charlie plays football too, mom. He was just named interim captain last week when a senior, Drew McCready, got his second concussion and was put on medical leave for the entire season." Kelsey's first thought was that, as a junior, this boy must really be a stand-out athlete on the football field. She thought he looked big enough. He didn't just have the height, he had the broad shoulders and thick build. Charlie, at eighteen years old, is one of the older students in his junior class.

"Well that's very impressive. Do you live here in Greenville?" Kelsey wondered if she knew of his parents. Bond High School fed into the surrounding cites so not every student enrolled lived in Greenville, New York.

"I live with my mom in the city, we've lived in the same penthouse since I was born. Our place is close to the bank where she works. Close enough for her to take the subway." Kelsey was taken aback. He couldn't be.

"Charlie, is your last name Thompson?" It wasn't just a small world, it was an amazing coincidence that this boy was standing in her living room eighteen years after he was born on the subway, given up immediately by his teenage birth mother and adopted by the single white female bank president who wanted a baby to complete her life. Her heart. Kelsey had never forgotten that story. She reported it. She wrote it. She photographed Baby Charlie, swaddled in a receiving blanket in his new mother's arms. It wasn't just a feel-good piece, and it was far from fluff. It was a story that tugged at your heart strings and made you believe in answered prayers. And miracles.

"Yes it is. How did you know?" Charlie looked confused and Bailey was just as curious about her mother's reaction to her new friend.

"You are Baby Charlie, born on the subway, and your mother – the beautiful Blair Thompson – was so gracious to allow me to interview her for the New York Banner all those years ago. I am a reporter, and your birth and your mother's story changed my outlook on life." Kelsey didn't elaborate but she will never forget it. The 'aha' moment for her, at twenty-eight years old, was when she quoted Blair Thompson saying, *"It feels as if the seams of my life have been let out just a bit."* That changed her. Without a doubt, Bailey Newman would not be in this life if it had not been for Kelsey chasing that feeling. Wanting and needing to feel seamless.

"That is amazing. So we've met before then, right?"

Charlie teased and then laughed, flashing his white teeth and contagious smile. Kelsey told him he was a beautiful baby then and now a very handsome young man. When Bailey and Charlie unpacked their backpacks on the coffee table in front of the couch in the living room, Kelsey left them alone to study. No boys were allowed upstairs in Bailey's bedroom, and Kelsey grinned at the thought of the look on Brady's face when he walks into the house later. A father never likes to see his teenage daughter show an interest in *liking* boys.

Kelsey wanted to know more about Charlie – and his mother. How was she doing? Was life treating her well? She obviously had raised a wonderful son to be proud of, both academically and athletically. Kelsey remembered Charlie saying that his mother still works at the bank. She was forty-five years old when Kelsey met her then, which meant she was now in her early sixties. Kelsey wasn't surprised that Blair Thompson was still a career-driven woman. She remembered her being smart, confident and youthful. And she probably still is. Her career had meant the world to her, until she found Charlie.

Brady walked through the kitchen doorway, interrupting her thoughts. Her husband was home, still wearing his scrubs from the hospital without any other layers. His arms were bare, and the cap sleeves on his shirt accented his biceps. She smiled at him as she turned away from the kitchen counter where she was chopping raw vegetables for a salad for dinner.

"Hey babe, you're a sight for sore eyes, you know that?" Brady had been working long hours at the hospital and Kelsey was missing him lately. Between her job as the editor of the Banner and taking care of and keeping up with the kids, life was busy. Six months had already passed since she and Brady had gotten married. His moving in and their life together wasn't just working, it was ideal, and they were happy.

Kelsey kissed him full on the mouth and then stuck a baby carrot in between his teeth. Brady laughed as he chewed, allowing his emotions to light up his bright crystal blue eyes, and the look he was giving her told her he wasn't thinking about food right now. "That will have to wait, hot stuff, your daughter has a guest in the living room. A study date."

Brady walked over to the doorway between the kitchen and the living room and peeked around the corner. "Who is that?" Just as Kelsey had expected, his eyes were wide and his expression was priceless. There was a teenage boy in the house, spending time with his daughter.

"He seems really nice. His name is Charlie and I actually have a story to tell you about how I know his mother, but that will be a topic during dinner. We are all eating together for a change."

***

During dinner, Kelsey told Bailey, Miles and Brady the story about Baby Charlie. Bailey playfully rolled her eyes each time her mother had called her big, strong, friend – a baby. Brady thought the story was incredible. He also knew all those years ago, at that time in Kelsey's life, she was in dire need of finding herself and truly living. And he had changed that for her. They had changed that for each other. He had never met anyone who made him feel and do things – anything – for the sake of love.

Chapter 2

Kelsey was fresh out of the shower in the downstairs bathroom, just off of her spacious bedroom that she now shares with Brady. Remodeling the downstairs to fit the needs of her and her new husband was a good idea, Kelsey had thought while blow drying her long dark hair, naked. The bathroom door was closed and this was her time. Her time to end the day having washed off the stress from work and the chaos of the evening at home with two kids – juggling homework, sports, and friends after school.

Her son Miles is eight years old, a third grader, and didn't care much about school. If it weren't for the basketball team at his grade school, he told his mom he really would not try so hard to keep Bs and Cs on his report card every quarter. Kelsey has been worried about her son lately. It's been six months since she remarried and bringing Brady into their lives has been positive. But it also has been a change. And kids are affected by change. Kyle's death greatly impacted – and changed – all of them. It's been two years since Miles lost his father but it was still so raw for him. Kelsey could see the rippling effect it was having on him, even now. Especially now.

Two nights ago, Miles missed the chance to score the winning shot at his grade school basketball game. There were four seconds left on the clock and he attempted to shoot – *just shoot* – Brady had yelled out from the stands. Miles was average in height for his age, but he could play basketball better than most of his peers. From the three-point line, the basketball had swiftly rolled around the rim twice and then fell off without going into the net. The home team crowd let out a disappointing groan as the buzzer sounded. The game was lost, and Kelsey could see that her son was feeling painfully disheartened.

As Brady and Kelsey walked down the bleachers to meet Miles after the game, his cell phone buzzed and he took a call from the hospital. He stepped away from the noise of the crowd filing out of the gymnasium as Kelsey found Miles in the middle of his friends on the gymnasium floor. She overheard one of the boys speaking to her son. "So who was the dude yelling out from the stands at you tonight?" And then another boy added, "He has been doing that a lot at our games." Miles bowed his head at first looking down at the floor, and then looked up at his teammates – *the guys* as he liked to call them at home – and said, "He's my step, um, he's my mom's new husband."

Kelsey wondered why Miles didn't want to call Brady his stepdad. Miles loves Brady. He seemed to really need a man in his life when Brady came back into Kelsey's life a little more than a year ago. She never asked him about Brady that night. She didn't want to embarrass her son in front of his *guy* friends, and she didn't want Brady to overhear them talking about him. The two of them still had not had that conversation, but Kelsey wanted to. She wanted to make sure Miles was feeling the love in their new family – and she also wanted him to know that he could talk to her about anything. Always.

She turned off the blow dryer and slipped on her favorite thick pink terrycloth robe, which had been hanging up on the hook attached to the back of the bathroom door. When she opened the door and walked into their bedroom, Brady was sitting up in their bed, waiting for her. The white flat sheet was pulled up to his waist, and Kelsey could see he was naked underneath.

"Happy to see me doctor, or does that thing always stand up and salute just anyone?" Kelsey giggled as she opened her robe and let it fall to the floor. She was naked, feeling confident and sexy, standing alongside the bed. Brady reached for her and pulled her down on top of him. She straddled him after he kicked the sheets off and down to the foot of the bed. Before their lips met, Kelsey asked in her quiet bedtime voice, "Is the door locked down here?" The two of them had to learn how to make love with kids in the house. Especially Brady. Kelsey had to remind him in the last several months how important it is for the kids not to overhear them. When she was married to Kyle, they were frequent lovers who knew how to keep the bed from squeaking, and to keep the moans silent. Brady was another story. An altogether different man. He lived in the moment. And he had been a bachelor all of his life.

"Yes it's locked," he assured her before he touched both of her breasts with his fingertips and then brought his mouth to her nipples, one and then the other. He sandwiched both of her breasts together with his hands and rolled his thumbs over her stimulated nipples. Kelsey was incredibly turned on as she put her mouth on his and kissed him passionately. She was still on top of him, teasing his erection with her body rubbing against his. It had been a few nights since the two of them were together like this, and it was time again. Time to find each other. Time to reconnect. A few moments later, Brady was on his knees and Kelsey had taken him into her mouth. He was muffling the sounds of pleasure that he wanted to express when there was a sudden knock on their bedroom door. Kelsey slid herself out from underneath Brady's legs and she grabbed her robe off the floor, quickly slipping into it, and tying it tightly around her body as she heard her son's voice from the other side of the locked door. "Mom, can I talk to you for a minute? Are you awake, mom?" Kelsey unlocked the door and opened it. Miles was standing there wearing a white short-sleeved undershirt, plaid pajama pants, and no socks. "Honey, what's wrong? It's late, you should be asleep," Kelsey didn't look back into the bedroom, in fear of her son seeing a naked Brady, as she walked out of the bedroom and into the living room area downstairs. She sat down on the couch and asked Miles to sit down beside her. "What's on your mind, little man?"Miles smiled at his mom's word choice, and God did he ever look like his daddy at that moment. Sometimes her son's expressions would throw her. It was Kyle. She missed him terribly, for herself, and for her children. Especially for Miles.

"I don't want to hurt your feelings, mom."

"Just tell me. I am a big girl, I can take it," Kelsey brushed his bangs away from his eyes. That sandy blond hair, just like his daddy's.

"I have a basketball game after school tomorrow and I don't want Brady to come." There it was. Kelsey knew she should have spoken to Miles about what she overheard at the last game. Did it bother him that Brady was an actively involved stepdad in the stands? Should she shush her new husband because Miles was feeling embarrassed? Kelsey had noticed how Brady had become more comfortable in his role as a stepdad. He was offering his opinion more – at home and especially at the kids' sporting events.

"I thought you liked having Brady at your games? I thought you loved having him in our family?"

"See – I knew you would be mad!"

"I am not mad, honey. Do I look mad?" She made a silly face and Miles giggled before she became serious again. "I need you to explain how you're feeling to me. Right now."

"Dad used to come to all of my games. He showed me the moves and taught me the rules here, at home, on our driveway. He saved his voice for our time. He never yelled out to me, or at me, during a game. He sometimes would stand up and pump his fists in the air, or give me a thumbs-up, but he never used his voice. He told me once that he didn't like when other dads were loud or obnoxious and he swore he would never do that to me."

"And Brady is doing that to you," Kelsey finished the words for her son, and he nodded. She expected to understand him when he came to her tonight. He is only eight years old. His problems were always simple and easy to solve. She knew what he was feeling when he began talking to her tonight. What she didn't expect, however, were the tears welling up in her son's eyes and escaping down his cheeks. "Oh honey, come here, stop. Don't cry," Kelsey pulled Miles into an embrace, trying to take away his pain and that is when she heard him quietly say, "I miss my daddy." She could have tried to find the right words at that moment. She could have tried to ease his pain and his sadness with encouragement, but instead she cried openly with her son and whispered, "I do, too."

After a few minutes had passed, the two of them regained their composure and Kelsey spoke to her son about the importance of coming together as a *new* family. Kyle was loved and would always be sorely missed. She reassured Miles how she wanted to hear more stories about Kyle that he had on his mind and carried in his heart. That is how they would keep his memory alive. Always. Just because she had a new husband now, did not mean she no longer loved his daddy – or missed him any less. But, Brady is in their lives now and he loves all of them as much as they love him. Brady would do anything for them, she said, including being a newly silent fan at Miles' basketball games from now on. Kelsey would see to that. Now she just had to convince Brady to change. Just a little.

***

When Kelsey walked upstairs with Miles, and tucked him into bed, she found herself looking at a framed photograph on his dresser. It was a photo of Kyle and Miles, which Kelsey had captured just weeks before Kyle died. She cropped it close in her camera lens to be able to see the similar features on their faces. Father and son. Kelsey knew their family was blessed to have a new life now, with Brady, but she also knew the deep wound from missing Kyle and their old life together as a family would never completely heal. Bailey appeared to have freely accepted the changes, maybe it was easier for her after having found out Brady is her biological father. The two of them were still so engrossed in the newness of their relationship. It warmed Kelsey's heart. And Kelsey is happy, too. She had always loved Brady and being married to him completed her in so many ways. Had he replaced Kyle? No. It was just different, as it had always been with Brady. And then there's Miles. He needed a man in his life, a father figure, and it appeared to be working out. And it will work out, Kelsey told herself as she ran her finger across Kyle's face in the picture and then turned off the lamp beside it and left her son's bedroom. She went back downstairs and when she walked into her bedroom, it was dark. Brady was in bed, and appeared to be asleep. Kelsey slid into the bed beside him after taking off her robe again. His back was to her when she reached for him, and that's when she felt him wearing his boxers.

"Hey… is it too late to pick up where we left off?" Kelsey asked him, and he turned onto his back.

Staring up at the ceiling, he asked, "What's going on with Miles?" His tone was serious and had sounded a little more hostile and a little less full of care and concern – and Kelsey was unnerved.

"He is worried about his game tomorrow." Would she tell him now? She knew she needed to. There would be no time to discuss this privately in the morning before work while getting the kids off to school. Then the game was scheduled immediately after school, and Kelsey and Brady were both planning to be there. "He's at that age where he gets embarrassed easily. He wanted to make that shot at the last game and when he didn't, he was crushed. Miles doesn't like a lot of attention in front of people, if you know what I mean. He doesn't like it when fans, or parents, yell from the stands. He is in the zone of playing ball and it bothers him."

"So everyone is supposed to sit quietly in their seats during the game so Miles doesn't get distracted or upset?" Brady was acting downright pissy.

"No, not everyone, just you." Brady sat up in bed and looked down at Kelsey lying there on her back. "Me? I'm the

14

reason Miles is upset tonight? What have I said?"

"You need to keep quiet at the games. His teammates have been asking him who is yelling at him from the stands."

"So he's embarrassed to have a stepdad now?"

"No. Not at all. Just be at the games and be supportive of him, but don't yell anything out to him."

"Oh for chrissake! You're going to make that kid into such a wus."

"Excuse me? *That kid* is my son, and he is a child. He has been through a tremendous loss and I thought you wanted to help see him through that and make a happy life for him."

"I'm going to sleep. I have an early day tomorrow." Brady plopped back down on the bed, fluffed his pillow, and turned his back to his wife.

"We all do. Goodnight. I love you, too." And that was all Kelsey said before calling it a day, and what had turned out to be a really difficult night.

***

Kelsey was waiting on the bleachers with a few other parents. It was fifteen minutes before game time and Brady was not there. She had not heard from him all day. Not even a single text which she had come to expect throughout the day, just to check in and say hello to his beautiful wife. He had showered and left the house before Kelsey had seen him this morning.

Their first real marital fight had left her stinging all day. She was angry at him for not getting it. Miles is just a little boy. Her boy. And Brady was acting like one of those incorrigible stepfathers. He was making her take sides. She was stewing that very thought and dwelling on how she would *always* be an advocate for her children. Against anyone. Maybe it was different with Bailey – because she is Brady's daughter and those who were close to them knew the truth now – but Miles deserved just as much love and understanding. As she focused on the clock high on the wall above the entrance, she brought her eyes down to the gymnasium floor and saw him walking in.

He had changed out of his scrubs and into a pair of long cargo khaki shorts and a hunter green t-shirt. It was hot outside in the August sun so he was wearing brown leather flip flops. At forty-six years old, he still looked as fit and as hot as men twenty years younger. Kelsey watched him climb the bleachers and sit down beside her, all the while exchanging hellos with the parents around them. Some were couples, some were just moms or dads alone who had made it out of work in time for an after school game.

"Hi babe," Brady said sliding close to her, putting his hand on her bare knee and gently rubbing it. She had not had time to change after work, so she was still wearing a melon-colored sundress with nude open-toe heels. Kelsey smiled at him, looked him straight in the eye, and said, "Hi yourself." Was he over it? Or was he just well aware that the other parents were very near and watching? Whether they were looking at them or not, they were watching. Many of the other mothers were Kelsey's friends and all of them had been very supportive of her when she remarried. Brady had been attending Miles' basketball games for over a year now. He had just become a little too comfortable expressing his excitement, or frustration, from the stands in the past few months since he officially became part of their family. Kelsey hoped that would change for the better today.

The entire game was a nail biter which kept the fans on the edge of their seats, and some out of their seats, as Miles and his teammates repeatedly bounced back and forth from taking the lead score against the opposing team. The final score was twenty-eight to twenty-six and this time Miles swooshed the last shot of the game into the net, breaking the ending tie – and winning for his team. Everyone was on their feet, cheering, and Brady was standing proud and tall, loudly clapping his hands together. He had not said anything more to her, or to Miles on the court, all throughout the game. When they walked together down the bleachers, they met a smiling Miles on the floor.

"Good game, buddy," Brady said, offering a fist pump to Miles and he returned it with enthusiasm. "Thanks Brady!" Kelsey just smiled at them both and willed away the tears welling up in her eyes. The two of them were okay. Again.

Chapter 3

Life resumed with very little conflict until Kelsey arrived home early from work a few days later and noticed Bree's car across the street, parked on the driveway. Kelsey had quickly gotten used to having her best friend in this life living right across the street. She and Jack Logan were living together and totally committed to each other and to raising Baby Sam.

Baby Sam was conceived by artificial insemination. When Bree lost her thirteen-year-old son, Max in a car accident, she quickly wanted to become a mother again. Jack Logan, a man she had worked closely with at an advertising firm for more than ten years, was there for her and committed to loving her and helping her raise a baby. He had never been able to impregnate a woman, but being sterile did not mean he could not be a father. His son, Sam Maxwell Logan, is now three months old.

Kelsey didn't bother to go inside her own house when she saw Bree's car at home. She walked across the street and knocked softly on her front door, just in case the baby was at home and asleep. Bree opened the door moments later, looking distraught. "What's going on?" Kelsey asked as she stepped up into the house and right next to Bree.

"I got a call from the daycare again. They can't handle him." Kelsey followed Bree into the kitchen and Bree told her to peek around the corner, into the living room, and when she did she saw Sam sitting in his baby swing, swinging swiftly, and fast asleep with a pacifier inside of his mouth. "His crying fits are so bad. I don't know what to do sometimes. I mean, the swing works or the vacuum and the kitchen vent sometimes calm him. He is just a fussy guy. The pediatrician says it's colic and he will outgrow it." Bree looked exhausted and a little hopeless. Kelsey walked over to her and hugged her close. "It is most likely just a phase. When you have a baby in the house, it's always something."

"Yes, so I've heard, but you're forgetting that Max was a star baby. I wanted four more like him," Bree giggled but felt a pang in her heart, thinking about her teenage son that she lost too soon.

"So why can't the daycare handle him? You can't tell me he's the first fussy baby to arrive there." Kelsey didn't envy Bree having to start all over with raising a child, dealing with all of the baby issues. Kelsey was more of a toddler mom. She liked to get down on the floor and play. Build those blocks, read a book, color that page. Cradling a baby and trying to figure out what all of the cries meant wasn't as enjoyable, for her. Kelsey had bonded with Sam a little in the last three months, and she was definitely trying to, but he was just a difficult baby all around.

"Well, they called me to let me know he had been crying for three hours and refusing to eat. I could have suggested the swing there again, and maybe they even tried it, but I just couldn't concentrate at work after that. I knew he needed me. So here we are. He never took his bottle after we got home, he just screamed and carried on until I put him in his swing on full speed and stuck the pacifier in his mouth. It took five minutes or so until he calmed down and zonked out." The last time baby Sam ended up in his swing after crying all morning it was a Saturday and he had slept, in motion, for four and a half hours. But those crying fits were happening almost every day now.

Kelsey was watching Bree and she could see on her face that she was torn. Her job, which she loved and excelled at, was now taking a backseat to her baby boy. "So this isn't the first time you've left work early to bring him home and calm him?"

"No. I've only been back to work for four weeks since my maternity leave, and I have yet to work a full five-day week. Thank God Jack is right there and able to cover for me – otherwise they would fire my ass." Jack is a good man, and he had always been there to rescue Bree over the years at the ad agency when she dealt with a personal problem. Now, however, her personal problem also was his. He came home to her and their baby at the end of every day. He was loving and understanding and very patient with Baby Sam. He just was not there enough to feel the extent of the frustration that Bree was dealing with, alone, most of the time.

"Oh honey, I wish there was more I could do. Why don't you and Jack take a break this weekend? Bring Sam over and I will watch him. Brady is on call at the hospital all weekend so we don't have any major plans and the kids will love having a baby in the house," Kelsey was hoping as she said those words that Sam would be in a good, happy mood. If not, the kids would ditch her and she'd be hauling out the vacuum to soothe him. Whatever she needed to do, she would do it. For Bree. Her dear friend needed to escape the stress of her new life for a few hours.

***

Those few hours turned into exactly seven hours, thirty-three minutes, and six seconds. That is how long Kelsey had spent trying to soothe Baby Sam. As expected, Brady was working and Bailey and Miles quickly made other plans with their friends when Sam, the fuss bucket, as Miles had dubbed him, came over for the day.

Kelsey had tried everything. Sam is familiar with her house. He knows who she is. *She's Aunt Kel who would do absolutely anything to make you stop crying at the very top of your lungs.* Bree and Jack brought over the baby swing and Jack set it up in the living room. All was quiet when they left the neighborhood. Bree was nervous and hesitant, but Kelsey nudged her out the door and told her not to worry, just have fun.

The multi-colored patchwork baby quilt was already spread out on the living room floor. Kelsey had found it in her keepsake chest downstairs. It had been both Bailey's and Miles' favorite quilt. She remembers them lying on it, sitting up on it, and just playing on the floor and exploring the toys around them. Even being mesmerized by the primary colors stitched into the patchwork quilt. Babies were so curious. Always learning.

Not Baby Sam though. Kelsey had been holding him when she closed the door behind his parents. She walked over to the quilt and bent over to place Sam down, on his belly. There were a few toys around him, including a rattle that lit up when you shook it, and a chew toy. Sam wanted no part of it. His body stiffened, his legs and arms were spread out in a stiff stance. His face was fire red, and after momentarily holding his breath, and then pressing his face into the quilt because he had difficulty lifting and keeping up his head, he started to cry. And never stopped. Kelsey quickly flipped him over to his back, but the damage had already been done. The quilt was the enemy now. She scooped him up and cradled him in her arms. She bounced him, she attempted to rock him in the rocking chair in the living room, and she walked him all through the house – up and down the two separate flights of stairs. Nothing worked. As soon as she would put the pacifier in, Sam would spit it back out. His face was still red and that redness spread itself all the way up to the roots of the little short blond hairs on his round, fair-skinned head. The stove-top vent in the kitchen, on high speed, worked for exactly two minutes and three seconds. The vacuum in one hand, being pushed around in Kelsey's bedroom with Sam in her other arm, had worked the longest. Exactly nine minutes and eleven seconds. Nothing soothed him for very long.

One half hour before Bree and Jack walked back into Kelsey's house, she had been successful at getting Sam to take a full bottle. My God, he was starving after resisting it all day long, and finally exhausted from crying. After he sucked the last drop of milk from the bottle, he fell asleep in Kelsey's arms. And she never attempted to move him. He was silent, and she was going to hold him in hopes of keeping him that way. When he slept, he looked just like his mommy. That boy is Bree's son alright. He resembled Max, too – and Kelsey had known that was both a comfort and a sad ache for Bree. Kelsey had thought how peaceful and content he *finally* looked snuggled up in her arms. If only she could have figured out, seven hours ago, what in the world was bothering him so terribly.

Bree was smiling and looking refreshed as she bent down to kiss Sam's cheek. "How was he? I texted you to check on him but you didn't respond." Kelsey hadn't heard her phone sound off, and she didn't doubt why.

"I told you he would be fine and not to check on him, and he was just fine." Why did mothers do that? Why was there an overwhelming need to protect each other from worry? Kelsey knew Sam was fine. He was not hurt or sick. He was just fussy. There was no need to share the crazy details with Bree. She would never leave her baby again if she knew. She was skipping out of work too much to rescue him from daycare. She had needed a break. And Kelsey gave it to her. And now Kelsey needed a glass of wine.

"Thank you for being here for Sam – and for knowing what I desperately needed," Bree said, carefully taking her baby from Kelsey's arms, and miraculously he kept sleeping while they talked and Jack folded up the swing and carried it back across the street to their house. Bree then swung the diaper bag over her shoulder and carried her sleeping son home.

Kelsey would ask her later, maybe sometime, if Sam prefers not to lie on his stomach. And maybe she would also bring up the fact she noticed he doesn't like to explore toys either. God love him, he is a handful.

***

Kelsey had just settled into her recliner with a full glass of her favorite White Zinfandel wine when Miles and Bailey filed into the front door. Bailey had driven them and two of their friends to the movies. She had now become a confident new driver at seventeen years old. She earned her driver's license when she turned sixteen, but she shied away from driving a car when Bree's son, Max was killed in a jeep driven by his teenage half sister. That accident, and that loss, had scared her, terribly. Months after, Brady was responsible for encouraging Bailey to get comfortable behind the wheel. And when she was, Kelsey gave her Kyle's vehicle. It was a silver 4 Runner that was five years old and in great condition as Kyle always kept his cars, and Bailey was honored to call it her own. It was just another piece of Kyle, the father she had known and loved since birth, for her to treasure.

"Is it safe to come in now?" Bailey asked as Miles crawled up into the recliner with his mom, and she carefully placed her wine glass on the table next to them so she wouldn't spill it.

"Oh Lord have mercy. What a day! Bree and Jack just brought him home," Kelsey sighed, not telling her kids how Sam had cried the entire time. She didn't want that information to get back to Bree, and quite frankly she just wanted to forget about it – and enjoy some peace with her family tonight.

***

As it turned out, Bailey had Saturday night plans with Charlie Thompson, again. That was happening frequently lately. And Miles wanted to order pizza and play video games. The leftover pizza was sitting in the box on top of the stove when Brady walked in the kitchen door and then into the living room where he found Kelsey sprawled out on the couch, sipping another glass of wine.

"Hey babe, rough day?" She looked tired, but he wasn't about to say it. He didn't want to tell her that she looked anything less than beautiful.

"Why? Do I look that bad? Is it that obvious Sam cried for seven point five fucking hours straight?" Kelsey sat up on the couch and ran her fingers through her hair. Brady's eyes widened. "You've got to be kidding me? He cried all day for you? Like nonstop screaming?"

"Pretty much," Kelsey whined, and Brady sat down beside her. He turned her body and rubbed her shoulders and then massaged his hands all the way down to the small of her back. She was tense, in knots, and he had sympathized with her having a rotten day. He knew though that she would do anything for Bree, and Bree obviously had needed to step out of the house and breathe for awhile. Especially if she was continuously handling Sam's fussing – day in and day out.

"So the pediatrician is calling that colic, huh?"Brady asked.

"That's what Bree said, and it does make sense, but–"

"But you think it's more than that?"

"I don't know. He flipped out when I placed him on his belly today. And he doesn't like toys. He isn't into exploring anything with his hands or eyes yet, maybe a little more so with his mouth. I just hope those things aren't red flags for something serious – and I don't know how to suggest that to Bree."

"Well the two of you have always been straightforward with each other about everything, so I think if anyone should mention this to her, it should be you. It may be nothing though. All babies develop and progress at different rates. Let's just wait and see, okay?"

"Okay," Kelsey forgot, for awhile, about worrying and trying to figure out and understand Baby Sam. Her husband was home for the night, and he and her kids were back on her radar.

Chapter 4

Kelsey was coming into the house, through the kitchen door, juggling three bags of groceries, when Brady met her in the doorway to help her carry. "Hey sexy, how was your day?" Kelsey asked him as she felt relieved to be home. She had worked late and then picked up a few groceries on her way home in case she had to cook dinner. She would first see what the kids had planned for the evening and if Brady was headed back to the hospital again. She was hoping for an excuse to not have to cook. It had been a long day, and she wanted to relax.

"Good. I mowed the grass after I got home from the hospital, and Miles and I played a few rounds of hoops before I told him he had to start his homework. So he's doing that now, in his bedroom, and Bailey left for a study date at Charlie's house." Brady had a concerned look on his face as Kelsey reacted. "She drove all the way back to the city to his penthouse? Has she been there before? You gave her permission to do that, huh?" Kelsey didn't know what to think. The drive back to the city was thirty minutes. She knew, because she drove it every day, and so did Brady. But at this time of the evening, the traffic was congested on the interstate. She didn't expect Brady to run everything by her that her kids wanted to do when she wasn't there, but this was new – and major.

"Yes, but Charlie was with her. He came home from school with her – apparently he didn't have a car today – and she basically was bringing him back home and they were planning to do their homework together, there." Brady felt nervous about the whole thing and he was ready for Kelsey to explode.

"Are you okay with all of that?" Kelsey asked him, surprisingly keeping her cool and feeling better about Bailey not driving alone. But she would have to come home, alone, later. And she was going to text her to make sure she left before dark.

"I don't know, babe. The driving part doesn't worry me as much as the boyfriend part." Brady was putting away a box of cereal in the cabinet above the wall oven and he looked back at Kelsey leaning against the sink with her arms folded across her chest.

"Boyfriend? Is that what she is calling Charlie now?" Oh Lord have mercy, it was time, Kelsey thought, to have a talk with her teenage daughter. A serious talk. About sex.

"Oh I don't know. She says they are friends, you know, but you and I both know what happens when an eighteen-year-old boy is alone with a seventeen-year-old girl. Ugh, babe, this new father thing is going to kill me." Kelsey couldn't help but giggle at him. He looked so forlorn. "It's not that bad. At least I don't think it is," Kelsey tried to reassure him, "Bailey is smart and mature, and she knows not to do anything irresponsible. I will talk to her later to find out what I can about what she and Charlie are up to." She walked over to Brady and hugged him close, and then he pulled her into a kiss. She kissed him back, long and slow and then a little more intensely. And when they parted, she smiled and said, "I think I have a forty-six-year-old husband who's going on eighteen."

He grinned mischievously and replied, "Watch it woman or I'll take you down to our bed right now."

"Ohhh, hold that thought for later."

***

Later, when Bailey pulled up onto the driveway, it was just beginning to get dark. She made it home safely. Kelsey had given her some time to shower and blow dry her hair and when she heard her daughter getting ready to go to bed, she walked into her bedroom after knocking on the door frame because the door was standing wide open. Kelsey still wasn't completely used to the fact that her bedroom upstairs is now Bailey's. It was the master bedroom she had shared with Kyle – and then later it was hers alone after he was gone. She missed the feel of being in that bedroom, as her own, and she loved the bay window that overlooked the backyard. Life was different now and sharing the basement with Brady had its perks. It was special, it was their space, and it allowed them privacy. Most of all though, it was good to make new memories with her new husband – away from the space and the rooms she shared with Kyle, the only man she thought she would ever call *her husband*. Kelsey pushed all of those current thoughts out of her mind, and sat on the end of the bed. Her daughter was already lying on it, reading a novel for an English literature class at school. She put her book down on her lap. "What's wrong mom? You have that *we need to talk* look on your face again."

"Nothing is wrong. I'm proud of you for being a safe, careful driver tonight. It was your first time driving into the city and all. And I'm glad you had Charlie with you so you weren't alone. So did you meet his mom tonight? And is their penthouse as glamorous as I remember?"

"The drive was fine. Brady prepped me for city driving months ago." Brady is her biological father, but Bailey and he had just found out that truth a year ago. Kyle Newman had raised and loved Bailey as his own, for fifteen years. He was her father and he was the man whom she called dad. She didn't know if she would ever be ready to call Brady, *dad*. He was hoping for that day to come. Kelsey was fine with Bailey calling him Brady. And Bailey wondered if there was something else she should call him. Pop maybe? Or *papa*, like French people say? Maybe not. It just wasn't very New York. "Yes, the penthouse is amazing, but I didn't meet his mom. She was working late at the bank."

"So you two were there alone? All evening?" Kelsey asked.

"Yes mom, Charlie and his mom are the only two people who live there."

"Bailey, you are seventeen years old – and I've been there – so I know how you have those crazy good feelings flowing through your body sometimes and you want to act on them. It's only natural for you to want to explore and experiment, but we need to talk about how far the two of you are going in this relationship. You're spending a lot of time together, alone and–"

"We're just friends, mom. Honestly, we are," Bailey said, very seriously. Kelsey has seen the two of them together and they did seem like close pals. They hugged frequently and laughed even more. "Charlie is not my boyfriend but he gets me. You know how much drama girls can bring into friendships and, well, I've never had a Bree in my life like you. I have girlfriends but not one close one. Charlie is new and different and it's just easy with him. He and I are getting really close." Kelsey appreciated her daughter's honesty, once again, and she was so grateful for Bree. The two of them shared a rare bond – and a special one at that. She had hoped one day her daughter would know exactly what it feels like to connect with another woman. There was nothing in the world like having a girlfriend to walk through life with – through it all.

"What's really close, Bay?"

"Friends. Close, like friends."

"Do you want to kiss him?" Kelsey asked and Bailey blushed.

"No, not like you mean. Not at all."

"Okay, well, if that changes, if your feelings for him change, I want you share that with me. I am here for you. Talk to me." Bailey had not yet had a serious boyfriend, and Kelsey hoped it would stay that way throughout her high school career. Too many young girls were losing their virginity just to be able to say they did it. There were regrets that went along with that kind of teenage behavior – and Kelsey wanted Bailey to feel special and loved for her first time.

"It's not going to change. Once you're gay you can't reverse it." Bailey spit the words out like she was talking about a change in the weather and Kelsey felt her eyes widen and her jaw drop.

"Gay? Um…Bailey?"

"No! Not me, mom. Charlie. Charlie is gay." Again, the nonchalant tone in Bailey's voice was unbelievable. It was comforting, Kelsey had thought for a moment. Comforting how kids nowadays accepted change, accepted different human beings in the world – and into their circle.

"Oh my gosh. I had no idea." Kelsey was a little shocked and very much relieved. She didn't need to worry about her seventeen-year-old daughter being ready for sex. At least not right now. Not with her new friend, Charlie.

The two of them talked a few more minutes about how grateful Bailey was feeling these past few months to have found Charlie. It was almost as if *he* was like a Bree in her life. They talked about *everything*, she said, and they *just get each other*, she added, smiling that infectious smile of hers and Kelsey reached for her daughter and pulled her into a tight hug. As she started to get up off of the bed, she wished her daughter a good night's sleep, and then Bailey spoke again.

"Mom, how old were you when it was your first time?" Kelsey stood up and looked directly at her daughter. There it was. The million dollar question some mothers and daughters never talked about. It just depended upon the type of mother you had. Was she old school? Was she one who had sworn off sex after forty because she just wasn't comfortable with her body that she had *let go* over the years? Was she a prude all of her life? Was she too embarrassed to share and to admit she was, in fact, a woman under that mother armor? Kelsey was not a single one of those types of mothers. Not even close.

"I was twenty-six years old and I was with your dad. Um, Kyle was my first." Kelsey still called him her dad because he was her dad. He was. "I know that seems *old* for a woman to first lose her virginity but quite frankly I was just not ready, or more importantly – I had not met the right man." Bailey was listening raptly as Kelsey continued to talk about herself – and her experience. She wasn't going to spell out the details of her sex life to her teenage daughter. She wasn't going to tell her that sex was so much better in her very late twenties, thirties, and even still in her forties. She was, however, going to tell her that it is okay to be true to yourself. And wait. "I had my first kiss in high school, and many more kisses on dates thereafter. I just never took off my clothes, all of my clothes, for just any man. I wanted to experience it, but I respected myself and my body enough to want that experience to be meaningful. And it was. Your dad and I fell in love and consummated our relationship soon after we met – because it just felt right."

"I love how you still continue to call him *my dad*. And I also love how honest you are being with me. It's comforting to know that you are a woman who isn't afraid to teach me good values. Mom, I think you're lucky to have loved and been with two wonderful men in your life. Um, you know what I mean, I know it was confusing for you when both dad and Brady were in your life… at the same time. I also know I am a product of that confusion." Bailey actually giggled and Kelsey tried to laugh too, but she felt nervous and a little ashamed. Still. And then she spoke. Straight from her heart.

"First of all – Kyle is your father, and he always will be. We are not changing that. Ever." Bailey smiled and tears filled her eyes. The pain of losing him was still so real. Kelsey immediately recognized that and reacted the same way, with tears in her own eyes. "And Bailey, you are not a product of confusion. You are a product of real love and real passion – and one day my greatest hope for you is to be as happy as I have been with both of the great loves of my life." Kelsey had hoped for all of that and so much more for her daughter. Didn't every mother? She knew every woman had a different story. It didn't really completely matter how anyone is raised. Life happened, everyone made choices, and lived with the consequences. Bree, for one, was promiscuous throughout high school and beyond. It doesn't change the fact that she is a wonderful, amazing person. It's just who she is. And, she has no regrets. She is even able to now, finally, talk about her ex-husband Nicholas Bridges – the father of her deceased son, Max – as a man she truly did once love with every fiber of her being. Their relationship was rocky from the start and all throughout their thirteen years of marriage, and now Bree was so much better off without him in her life. Without him though, they never would have given life to their son. And Bree would not trade that time for anything. Because then, she had her boy. Alive and well. And in her life.

When Kelsey went downstairs to go to bed, she found Brady working intently at his desk in the den. He had some research to do and he often liked to bring that work home so he didn't have to stay too late at the hospital. Kelsey walked in and he looked up at her with a wide smile that lit up his eyes. God he loved her, as she loved him, so much. "Ready for bed are ya?" he asked as she sat down on the edge of his desk in front of him.

"Getting there," she responded, "I just had an interesting conversation with Bailey."

"Uh oh, do I wanna hear about her romance with Charlie?" Brady seriously felt frazzled at the thought of his daughter coming into her own, becoming a woman. He had just found her, and he wanted to keep things as they are for awhile. Even though Bailey isn't a little girl and he never knew her as a child, he just wasn't ready to see her grow up too fast – and to have to share her with a boy she *liked*.

"Well it turns out it's not a romance. They are close friends and it's going to stay that way – because Charlie is gay." Kelsey waited for Brady's response. She grinned when she got it and then laughed out loud at him. He sat upright quickly in his big black leather swivel chair with inner cushions made for a couch. "What? Yes! That is the best news a father could ever hear! I knew I liked that boy!" He was especially fond of *that boy* now knowing he wouldn't be inappropriately putting his hands anywhere on his daughter. When Kelsey finished giggling, she told Brady how surprisingly comfortable it was to talk to their daughter about sex. She admitted to initially feeling uneasy, but having the truth out in the open after all these years has helped her to teach Bailey it is okay to follow your heart – but so very important to use your head.

"Well I'm proud of you for being one of those women who can talk to your daughter, our daughter, about your own life experience. I really think it helps when a child, or a teenager, can get a genuine feel for how their parent is a real human being – not just a mom or a dad. I never had that. I was six when my mother died and my father was lost to me after that. I learned about sex from the guys in the locker room at school and the porn we rented at the neighbor kid's house." They laughed together as Kelsey tried to picture Brady growing up. She felt sorrow knowing he was so alone and had to feel his way through life like a blind person amid a crowd of unfamiliar surroundings.

"You're a good man, Brady Walker. You turned out exceptionally well – and I'm proud to call you my husband." Kelsey leaned forward and took his face into her hands. He had some stubble growing at the end of the day since his early morning shave. It never took him long to grow stubble. By tomorrow morning, his face would be scruffy. And that scruffy face always reminded Kelsey of the first time she met Dr. Brady Walker.

"I am grateful for every day you are in my life," Brady said, wrapping his arms around her waist. "I love you and our kids more than you will ever know." Brady was speaking from the heart and Kelsey teared up and kissed him long and hard on the mouth, and when she stopped he was beaming and they were both thinking and feeling the same thing. Kelsey walked over to close – and lock – the office door. It was time to see just how durable that big, comfortable, chair is in his office.

Chapter 5

The career program at Bond High School was slow to take off. The original plan, devised by a team of teachers, was to have the sophomore students choose a career in which they are interested in pursuing – and then meet with actual professionals to learn the trade. It was intended to give the students a head-start on making decisions, choosing a path or specialization in preparation for college, and then work hands-on in a job-shadow format. Senior year came soon enough for high school students and the idea to start early, as sophomores, seemed like a smart one. All of those students were placed last school year with a professional in a specific field. Workshops were conducted at school, weekly, and some of the students – who were serious about their interest in a chosen profession – were benefitting from the program. Those students were now juniors and the career program was about to take a new turn. Before that happens, however, all of the students who were still actively involved in the career program – those who had not dropped out, or wasted other people's time in order to get out of going to class – were instructed to decide whether they wanted to be in, or out. Because it was finally internship time.

This quarter, each professional had chosen one student from their group to take part in doing an internship at their workplace. The mentors and the students had gotten to know each other and learned from each other over the past year. Some of the students were most definitely interested in pursuing specific careers now. Those were the students whom the teachers were allowing to move forward first in the career program and complete an internship. Internships were designed for college students so the teenagers at Bond High School were extremely excited to be given this early opportunity. Bailey Newman is one of them.

Bailey and Brady had met for the first time at Bond High School, a year and a half ago, when Bailey decided she wanted a career in the medical field. After high school, she was going to attend college and study to become a doctor. She, however, had not been entirely sure what type of doctor. Brady was then the new chief of staff at Laneview Hospital in New York City, and he had volunteered to work with the high school students. It was something he felt he could do to give back to the community. When he met Bailey, he initially had no idea she was the daughter of Kelsey Duncan – his former lover and the woman, for him then, who was *the one that got away.* When Brady made the connection that B. Newman, as printed on his attendance sheet on the first day of the career program, was Kelsey and Kyle Newman's daughter – he couldn't believe it. She did look so much like her mother, and he immediately welcomed the chance to teach her the ropes of medicine. And maybe somehow make his way back into her mother's life.

When he asked her what her first name was, *what did the B stand for,* he was stunned. Bailey was his mother's name. The mother he lost, to pancreatic cancer, when he was a six-year-old little boy. He had told Kelsey all about the woman who was the beacon in his world – before she left him too soon – and he had told her, his mother's name. It was many months later when Brady learned that Bailey is, in fact, his biological daughter. His and Kelsey's affair had resulted in a baby girl. Bailey Newman is his, and she was raised, loved, and adored by another man. Kelsey married Kyle Newman and she kept her baby's paternity a secret for nearly sixteen years. Kyle died of a brain aneurysm when Bailey was fifteen years old, and soon after her biological father came into her life – and back into her mother's – the secret was revealed. It was almost as if it had been written for a storybook. Bailey lost one amazing father – and had gained another. Her life just wasn't as sad anymore with Brady in it.

Like her mother, she worshipped Brady. She, so easily, could get caught up in him. And she was. Their connection began with the career program when they bonded over medicine. And today was the first day of Bailey's internship at Laneview Hospital, working alongside Dr. Brady Walker. Her father.

Bailey was the first to get showered and be downstairs for breakfast. It was early October and there was a chill in the house as she made her way through the living room and into the kitchen wearing pajama pants, a sports bra, and her open robe over top. Her feet were bare and feeling chilly but she didn't want to go all the way back upstairs for a pair of socks. After she helped herself to a toasted bagel with light butter, she sat down at the table as her mom walked into the kitchen. "Well good morning sweet thing, that looks good." Kelsey said giving her daughter a kiss on top of her head and checking out the warm bagel on her plate.

"Hi mom, I'm so pumped about today, I just wanna get ready and go! Is Brady getting ready?" Brady was always up and ready before them and sometimes already at the hospital for the day.

"He is downstairs in his office and will be ready when you are." Brady was waiting to take Bailey with him to the hospital for the entire day. He was excited too, and he told Kelsey just how much before they went to sleep last night. This was an opportunity for him and his daughter to bond further. They both felt the same pull to the make a difference. To be a doctor. Soon after they began working closely in the career program, Brady helped Bailey narrow her interests and she had chosen to study pediatrics. She had not changed her mind since. And that, in part, is what the career program was designed to do – put a student in the environment and see what happens. If they love it, they will excel. If it's not for them, there is plenty of time to explore other options. Even before college.

Brady is not a pediatrician. He is a brain specialist, and a surgeon. He is qualified to serve as a general practitioner and general surgeon when needed, and he does. Following medical school, he spent years working in the emergency room at Laneview Hospital. He had seen and worked with it all. And he was confident he could handle it all, too. Today, with Bailey, he had arranged his schedule so he would be working among the emergency room doctors in the morning – and then making rounds to check on the recovery and the progress of his brain trauma patients in the afternoon. Some were hospitalized, and some had appointments to see him. Bailey would be alongside of him for all of it. He wanted her to see the performance of various doctors. The introduction to pediatrics would come later.

"I can't wait mom! What am I going to wear though? I need to see if Brady thinks I should dress up." Bailey was putting her plate in the sink while speaking to Kelsey who had sat down at the table with a glass of orange juice. And that's when Brady walked into the kitchen, already dressed in royal blue scrubs for the day with matching Nike tennis shoes. He was carrying a hanger with clothes on it, with a white plastic covering over top. Bailey thought he had some dry cleaning. But then he handed it to her.

"This is just a little something for you as we begin a journey together today." Brady was smiling and Kelsey was enjoying seeing the two of them together, like this. Bailey took the hanger from him and pulled off the plastic. She had her own set of scrubs, in aqua.

"Oh Brady! My own scrubs!" She grabbed him around the neck with one arm and planted a kiss on his clean-shaven cheek. "I just love you to pieces. Thank you for these!" Brady gave her a squeeze, told her he loved her more, and when she said she was going to go upstairs to put them on, Kelsey was dabbing her eyes with a napkin that Bailey had left on the table.

"The two of you warm my heart when you're together like that," she told her husband, "I can only imagine how much she is going to learn from you at the hospital. You're a gem for doing all that you've done, and now this too."

Brady bent over the table and kissed her on the mouth. "It's my pleasure. I'm the lucky one." And Kelsey knew what he meant. He didn't speak of it too often but he had expressed his gratitude for finally knowing the truth. He never would have known had Kelsey not witnessed their bond and wanted to tell them. It had felt strange for him to feel a need to thank her for her honesty – because for fifteen years she had lied to him and kept his daughter from him. It was awkward too for Kelsey, but that was in the past now. It had to be. They were all enjoying the present, united as a new family, and looking forward to the future. All together.

***

The day at the hospital started off hectic in the emergency room. Brady was amazed at how Bailey did not seem to be affected by all of the blood from the gunshot victim's leg, the severed finger from the five-year-old little boy who was playing in his father's workshop in their home garage before school, and the panic in the eyes of the sixty-year-old heart-attack victim. She was right there, alongside of him, as he tended to the needs of each patient. She helped when she was asked, and she observed every single second before, during, and after. When their morning shift in the emergency room was finished, Brady asked her if she wanted to get something to eat in the cafeteria for lunch – before his rounds began with his patients. As the two of them were walking together down the hallway, one of the nurses caught up with them.

"Dr. Walker…" Brady and Bailey both stopped and turned around. "Your twelve-thirty appointment canceled for today, so I wanted you to know that you can take your time with lunch – with your daughter." Mary Sue smiled sweetly at Bailey. A heavy-set woman, sixty-two years old, with bright red shoulder-length hair and a round face full of freckles, had been working at Laneview Hospital for thirty years and worked alongside Dr. Walker the first time when he had been on staff more than fifteen years ago. She liked him, as a person and as a professional, and she was happy to have him back. She remembered when he met and fell hard for the young girl's mom. She, and a few others still on staff, couldn't believe when he told them he had a daughter. They knew she was from *that* relationship which began at Laneview Hospital all those years ago. They just couldn't believe Dr. Walker had never known. Because he had never been told. He only confided in a select few of them with the truth, because he knew Bailey would be there at the hospital working with him throughout her internship – and he was too proud not to tell them she is his daughter. It didn't matter though. You tell one nurse, you tell them all. Gossip spread like wildfire in those hospital hallways, but who cares? At least Brady didn't.

Bailey was surprised to hear the nurse call her *his daughter*. She felt a little uncomfortable, but people were going to find out eventually. She was feeling disloyal to Kyle – and she wondered if that would ever get any easier. She had mixed emotions sometimes.

The two of them found a table in the back of the cafeteria after Brady bought a couple of turkey sandwiches, two cups of broccoli cheese soup, and bottled water. "Sorry if the food selection isn't the greatest here." Brady wasn't exactly sure what Bailey liked to eat yet. He was still learning things about her. He knew she, like her mother, ate healthy and watched her portion sizes – and looked great because of it. He also knew she liked to indulge in a good pepperoni pizza once a week or so, just like her mother.

"Oh this is fine. I eat in a cafeteria every day at school, remember?" Bailey giggled, and then Brady reminded her that he lives with her – and sees her make her lunch to take to school at least a few days a week.

"So does it make you uncomfortable how people are beginning to find out who you are, to me, here?"

"Um, no. I just want this experience to be professional. I don't want anyone to think I fell into it because I am the doctor's daughter. I feel like I deserve this chance." Brady smiled at her. She was so grown up and a lot like her mother in so many ways. She worried about what other people thought of her.

"You *do* deserve this chance. Don't worry about anyone here. You make me proud and they know it – and that is all I care about. I love you and I am looking forward to more days and more moments like this with you. You are a natural already. You were born to be Dr. Bailey…" and he hesitated before saying it, "Newman." He wondered if she would ever want to take his name. She was, after all, by blood, his blood, a Walker.

And it was as if she was reading his mind, but she didn't go there. She wouldn't go there. She was born Bailey Newman and she would keep her name until one day, if and when, she got married, then she would take her husband's name. She liked her name. And it was just another piece of *him* that she could hold on to. Kyle Newman was her dad. Brady was, well, just Brady. He was more to her than her mother's husband, or just a stepdad. She loved him, but she couldn't take his name, or call him dad. Not yet anyway.

When the conversation turned back to medicine and the rush from the morning they had shared, Bailey began to feel comfortable again. Less pressure. At the same time, Kelsey was just leaving work. It was noontime and the pressure, for her, to meet the newspaper publication deadline was over and she was taking the rest of the day off. It was a sixty-five degree October day and she wanted to go home and go for a run. Sometimes her gym workouts, after working all day, had to take a backseat to her family. She never lost sight of staying fit though. She always managed to run a few times a week, whether it was outside or on the treadmill. Running had always been good for her body, and her mind. She didn't have anything in particular weighing on her mind today – she had just been thinking about life. Its challenges. And its blessings. She was wondering how the day was going with Brady and Bailey at the hospital. She hadn't heard from either one of them, and decided it would be more fun to wait and hear their story – and see their faces – at home tonight.

***

Kelsey was pounding the pavement. She was finishing up her four-mile run and feeling the pull in her calves and the tightness in her stomach. It was a good hurt, but she was relieved to be just blocks away from her home. She wasn't thinking about anything or anyone in particular when she focused on the man walking up ahead of her, pushing a stroller. It was Jack Logan, and Sam.

Sam, at almost six months old, was propped up inside of the jogging stroller and appeared happy and content with his ride. Until it stopped. When Jack stopped to talk to Kelsey, Sam wailed. He wanted more movement. "It's okay buddy, we will move in a minute." Jack started rolling the stroller in a back and forth motion, which seemed to sooth Sam momentarily. And that's when Kelsey noticed Jack was wearing his dress clothes, for work. He had on his black suit pants, a white dress shirt, and a powder blue tie loosened up around his neck. In the sunlight, his brown hair was showing shades of gray and a few lines on his face appeared around his eyes when he squinted. He is an attractive-looking man, in his mid fifties, and his six-foot frame carried very little body fat.

"What's going on?" Kelsey asked, turning off the music on her iPhone and pulling the white earbuds out of her ears.

"I know, I'm too fancy for an afternoon stroll," Jack joked, and then explained, "Sam had a rough morning at daycare again and when Bree got the phone call at work, she was a minute away from starting a presentation with a potential new client."

"So you saved her." Yet again, Kelsey thought. Jack Logan was a godsend to Bree. Kelsey knew that Bree truly loved Jack, and she was around frequently enough to be an eye witness to the two of them making it through Sam's rough babyhood together, and growing stronger because of it.

"Well I tried to reassure her that Sam would be fine at the daycare, and he would get past his fit of the day again, but Bree wanted to rescue him. I am in between meetings so I convinced her to work while I take care of Sam for a couple hours." Kelsey looked at Sam who was chewing on his pacifier he found inside of the stroller. He was a mystery sometimes. An emotional wreck one minute, and smiling and laughing the next. "Jack, I can watch him if you need to get back to work." Kelsey wanted to spend some time with Sam. He was well-behaved for her *sometimes*, and even if he wasn't happy – Kelsey was feeling up for the challenge today.

"No. I don't want to take up your time on your day off."

"You won't be – Sam will be, and I love me some Baby Sam," Kelsey smiled, took the stroller from him, and Jack laughed and thanked her.

"I will let Bree know. Feel free to grab some of his things at the house and take him back to yours if that is more convenient for you. His bottles are in the fridge." Jack bent down and kissed his boy on top of the head and told him goodbye before he headed back toward his house to get his briefcase and his car, and Kelsey decided to take Sam for a long walk before taking him home.

***

Sam was a good boy, happy and content for the next two hours. Kelsey fed him his bottle over at his house. While doing so, she noticed he was still having difficulty with holding his own bottle. After she fed Sam, she found the diaper bag and took him over to her house. When she turned on the television for him, The Little Einsteins were playing on The Disney Channel, and Sam seemed to like watching that while Kelsey was holding him. Since he was happy, she decided to set him down on the carpeted floor four or five feet in front of the couch. But as soon as she placed him into a sitting position, Sam threw himself back. He didn't hit his head on the couch, but he came close. She tried again, placing him farther away from the couch this time, but he wouldn't sit up. He wasn't upset, he just appeared lazy and wanted to lie down on the floor, flat on his back. Kelsey allowed him to stay how he was comfortable and he was still watching the same show when Bree knocked once and walked in the front door. Kelsey watched Sam's face light up when he saw his mommy, and Bree too was looking equally as happy to see her baby boy when she picked him up off of the floor.

"Thank you so much for doing this. Jack was just as busy as I was today, but he knew I needed to snag that new client. He told me you volunteered to help – so now I hope you know he adores you as much as I do!" Bree was smiling as she walked over and hugged Kelsey with Baby Sam content on her hip.

"You don't have to thank me. It was deadline this morning and then I decided to take the afternoon off. And for what it's worth, I adore you, your man, and your little man." There was no engagement ring or wedding talk as of late between Bree and Jack. Their lives were consumed with Sam and his high maintenance nature. One day, however, the two of them would seal the deal. They were both sure of it.

"So how was he? Did he enjoy being outside?" Bree had turned into one of those mothers who could not think of anything else but her baby. And Kelsey understood her desire to make sure all is well in his little world. The problem is, and continued to be, Sam is rarely happy or content.

"He was super! He was a star today. I wish the weather would be this beautiful every day because he loves to be in that stroller, and moving," Kelsey smiled at the thought of having to stop for traffic when she was crossing the street with Sam. He threw himself back into the stroller and kicked and fussed until the cars passed and Kelsey began walking with him again.

"Oh good! Mommy is so proud of you. Now if we could just get you to like daycare." Sam didn't look like he was listening to Bree's words. Or, it seemed as if he didn't fully understand what she was saying. He was making fleeting eye contact as Bree was talking to him and then she kissed his chubby cheeks, one and then the other, as Kelsey plopped down on the couch.

"Sit a minute or two. He likes this show," Kelsey offered, and Bree also tried to place Sam in a sitting position on the floor. He repeated the same scenario of throwing himself back and then finding comfort flat on his back. Kelsey noticed how Bree sat him back up and propped him against the base of the couch in front of her feet after she sat down. Sam slid away from that support and once again found his back – flat on the floor. "Oh, okay, you don't want to sit nice today?" Bree tried to laugh it off but Kelsey saw the concern in her eyes.

"Why do you think he does that, Bree? He doesn't like to sit, and he cannot independently get into a sitting position yet. Have you thought about mentioning that to your pediatrician?" Kelsey was trying to be careful with her word choice, but she wasn't tip toeing around the subject either. This is Bree she is talking to. The two of them could always speak their minds to each other. About anything.

"He has his six-month check up next week. I'm concerned about that, and so many other things," Bree sighed and glanced over at Sam flapping his hands in mid air while The Little Einsteins were singing on the TV. Sam was excited to watch and listen, the music had his complete attention. Kelsey scooted closer to Bree on the couch and reached for her hand. "He could be a little delayed, all babies are different. I'm sure he will be fine, but having a proactive mama is going to see him through any rough patches in his life," Kelsey meant those words. Bree had changed since Sam's birth. Life wasn't all about her anymore. She had been very present and a good mom to her son, Max for thirteen years. But, then, he was easy and Bree could still have a life, outside of being a mother. She had a career she could concentrate on. Life certainly wasn't easy now. She had wanted a baby to get back into living – after Max's death – but now this baby was her only life. He consumed her. She wasn't enjoying his babyhood, she felt as if she was rushing it. Rushing through the days and nights. *Maybe tomorrow will be better? And sometimes it was.* Rushing the months until he would reach a milestone. *Maybe next month he will be able to sit up on his own?* He most definitely consumed her, because he was needy, worrisome, and fussy. And she was there for him. No matter what he needed. She was there.

Minutes later, Sam was sprawled out on the floor, sound asleep. His body looked completely relaxed for a change. He appeared peaceful, instead of rigid and uncomfortable. Kelsey grabbed his fleece baby blanket from the chair in her living room and covered him. "Let him sleep there for awhile. Are you hungry? Or should I get us some wine?"

"Oh get the wine, sweets," Bree smiled and the two of them kept their laughter quiet on purpose.

***

An hour later, Sam was still asleep on the floor and Bree was feeling so much better with a buzz. "It's three-thirty in the afternoon and we're borderline drunk," she giggled and Kelsey squeezed her knee, and said, "Oh, no, just a little looped that's all."

"Can I ask you something, Kel?" Bree suddenly felt serious, the wine was making her more open to speaking about her feelings. And her fears as of late.

"Anything. You know that."

"What am I going to do if there is something wrong with my baby? What if these first few months with him are setting the stage for a life of, I don't know, special needs…" There. She had said it. They had all been thinking it. And wondering about it. Wondering what if Bree's baby has real problems, real challenges? That would be life changing. But hadn't he already changed their lives? And they were dealing with it. And that was the answer Kelsey had for her.

"We do not know if there is anything *wrong* with Sam," Kelsey said, "This may just be a rough start and he may flourish in the coming months and you will never look back. This is something you need to take one day at a time – and mention your concerns to his pediatrician."

"I just can't shake the feeling that he's not normal," Bree was crying and wiping her cheeks as the tears streamed down, "I'm scared, Kel. I'm scared for him – and I'm scared for me. I'm not designed that way. I can't handle what other people endure when their babies have, uh, I can't even say it again. I can't even say *special needs* without cringing. How terrible am I?" Bree was still crying, and Kelsey wanted to join her. She also had all of those same thoughts – for her dear friend whom she loved like a sister – because there have been many red flags in Sam. Nothing was terribly alarming, but still obvious something was not quite right.

"First of all, you *are* handling it. Don't you see? You are being the mommy that your baby needs, regardless of what his needs are. Bree, you are loving him and doing your darndest to understand him. You will see him through whatever lies ahead." Kelsey was tearing up but she wanted to be strong. "Someone told me something once, and I know I've never shared this with you. If we all were to hang up our problems on a clothesline for everyone to see and then be given the choice to take down any problem, any at all, we would all take back our

55

own problem…because we know we can handle it."

"Wow. I think you're right about that. I just feel so overwhelmed sometimes," Bree said, slipping her arm through Kelsey's, sitting next to her on the couch, and she finished off her third glass of wine. "So, who told you that?" Bree asked and Kelsey smiled as she felt a flood of goodness inside of her body. "Someone I still carry in my heart."

"Kyle," Bree said, giving her a soft smile, "You miss that sweet man, don't you?" Kelsey wished she had more wine in her glass which was sitting empty on the table next to couch. "Yes, and I always will. It doesn't go away." Bree understood her words and her feelings all too well. Missing Max was a similar, familiar pain.

"I know I shouldn't ask you this because I know myself how Sam has not replaced Max in my life. I never intended for him to. I just wanted to ease the pain. Has Brady eased the pain of losing Kyle, and missing Kyle? Are you happy being remarried?" That was a loaded question and Kelsey was not even sure how to begin to answer it. Her life did feel complete. Her children are healthy and happy and actively involved in their schools, in sports, and with their friends. And Brady is a supportive, loving *dad* to both of them. And he is a wonderful husband to her. She loves him. Oh how she loves him, but not with her whole heart. That just could never be.

"I am very happy with Brady. He has been there, just as he promised he would be, for me and for my kids. Our physical attraction is beyond amazing, and we connect and get each other on every other level too. He's the man for me now. And always."

"But...?" Bree could hear in Kelsey's voice how there was more weighing on her mind.

"But my kids come first, and I think Brady struggles with that sometimes. Is being married to me everything he thought it would be? I don't know. My life is different now, since he and I reconnected. I have responsibilities. My weeknights are all about my kids and their activities – and we try to reserve the weekends for family time. Bailey is getting older and naturally she likes to put her friends first, and that is okay because life changes. I know Brady, the bachelor, has had a lot of adjustments to make, living with us, and being a family with us. But I feel like it's working, minus a few glitches here and there."

"Yeah it's like I told you a long time ago – life gets in the way sometimes but if we really want to make it work we just deal with it – and eventually, hopefully, overcome it. And I guess I should take my own advice. Just start taking things one step at a time with Sam and not worry so much about what lies ahead." Bree was feeling better already, having had the time to talk, really talk, to Kelsey. "So tell me more about bedding him every night in the basement..." Bree laughed loudly, too loud, at her own comment and Sam began to stir.

"Listen to yourself, you're asking *me* about sex? You're the one I've taken coaching from for over half my life," Kelsey giggled as they watched Sam open his eyes and stare at the ceiling, trying to remember his surroundings as he began to look side to side.

"Hey it's been too long, okay? Jack and I are beat by the time we do hit the sheets every night," Bree was whining and Kelsey was smiling at her.

"Hang in there, Bree. It's just a phase," Kelsey teased her. And then Sam cried, stiffening his arms and legs again. He woke up unhappy. Unhappy with the world around him. A world his parents are slowly and carefully trying to introduce him to, but all they are getting in return from Baby Sam is resistance.

Chapter 6

One week later, Kelsey was staring at her desk calendar at the newspaper office. It was deadline again, it was Bailey's day at the hospital with Brady again, and it was Baby Sam's six-month check-up with the pediatrician. Deadline would be met in a couple hours, Bailey's day would probably be even better than last week – considering she is certain she has found her calling – and Bree hopefully will be getting some much-needed guidance for how to help Sam. Time has not been on Bree's side. Sam wasn't *outgrowing* anything. His issues were ongoing and believing it was *just a phase* was appearing more unlikely with each passing day.

Kelsey pushed her thoughts back to writing a headline for a front page story when she noticed a stack of piled messages on the corner of her desk. *While you were out: The mayor called; Check with Mike in advertising about next week's special lay out; Call Taylor Barton, 555-212-8772.* Kelsey didn't recognize the name Taylor Barton and the area code for her phone number was not in New York. She set her messages aside just as the intercom on her phone sounded. It was Madison, the secretary in the main office at the newspaper. "Kelsey, you have a call on line two. Taylor Barton."

"Do people not know I'm on deadline?" Kelsey teased and Madison giggled before hanging up. Kelsey knew this was the second phone call to her from Taylor Barton, someone she didn't know, but it is the norm for her to receive phone calls from strangers for story ideas, or compliments and complaints about the Banner.

"This is Kelsey Walker." She had her office phone tucked between her ear and her shoulder as she typed a headline idea on the computer screen.

"Hi, this is Taylor Barton, um, you do not know me. I am from Washington, D.C. and I'm in New York for a few days and I would like to arrange a meeting with you, if you have time for me." Kelsey stopped typing, took the phone off of her shoulder, and sat up straight in her chair. "Does this concern a possible story? If you can give me a little insight, I will know which of my reporters to give this assignment to. I am the editor here at the Banner so most of my time is not spent reporting, or writing."

"I don't want to meet with anyone else," Taylor said, "I'm not looking to be interviewed. I came to New York City to talk to you."

"Why me?" Kelsey asked, thinking that was odd.

"My sister was Joanie Sutter. She died of breast cancer ten years ago – when she was involved with Brady Walker, um, your husband now." Kelsey's jaw dropped. She knew about Joanie. Brady had told her. She didn't know her last name was Sutter. She did know that Brady and Joanie were engaged to be married, but Joanie had lost her battle with breast cancer just months before their planned wedding date. Brady never spoke about her, and Kelsey had not cared to ask any questions about her or his life with her. That was a time in their lives when they were apart. She was happily married then to Kyle with two children and a complete life. She had wanted Brady to move on, without her, and he tried, he told her. Kelsey remembered Brady talking about being beside himself when he could not save this woman – he had loved her and wanted to move on with his life, with her. She was a nurse at the same hospital in Washington, D.C. where Brady was hired when he left Laneview Hospital in New York City. "You may not even know about Joanie–" Taylor began to speak again on the phone because Kelsey continued to be silent. She was thinking and remembering, but didn't have any idea why this woman's sister is calling her. A lot of years had gone by since her sister's death and Brady's involvement with her. *And what do I have to do with any of this?* Kelsey thought to herself before finally speaking. "I do know who she was. I've only heard of your sister by her first name though. You said her last name was Sutter?"

"Yes that was her married name. Our maiden name is Stuart."

"Married name? So your sister was married before?" Kelsey felt awkward. This conversation was strange. Why would she want to talk to the sister of her second husband's former lover? Or, more importantly, why is Taylor Barton contacting her?

"Yes she was, but Marty died." There was sadness in Taylor's voice, and Kelsey kept thinking, *Lord have mercy,* the world was just full of death and dying. Too much of it. She still felt sadness for people she didn't even know when family or friends died young. It just didn't seem right to print obituaries week after week in the newspaper if the dead were not old. Take those people who are old and ready. *My gosh, it just hurts too much, still, to think about losing Kyle.* "Listen, Kelsey, I really do not want to get into anything on the phone. I know you're working and probably terribly busy – but do you think you can find the time to meet with me in the next couple of days? I have a flight scheduled to go back to Washington D.C. on Friday morning."

"Um, yes, I suppose we could meet this afternoon, after my deadline, or maybe first thing tomorrow morning?" Kelsey was looking at her desk calendar again.

"This afternoon would be good, thank you for making time for me," Taylor responded.

"Okay sure, how about one fifteen?" Kelsey suggested to

her. "Do you want to come to my newspaper office or meet somewhere?"

"I am not very familiar with New York City, but I can take a cab from my hotel to wherever you want to meet."

"Tell the cab driver the Café on the Corner, on Fifth Street. That restaurant is just blocks away from my office and I will be ready for a break from here by then. Okay with you?"

"Yes. I will see you there, later," Taylor said, and Kelsey hung up the phone feeling a little confused and maybe even a little intrigued. But that was only because she was born curious. She was, after all, a seasoned reporter now. This woman obviously has something on her mind, but exactly what Kelsey has to do with any of it remained to be seen. She forced herself not to continue thinking about it. She had to get back to work.

***

At one-o'clock, Kelsey walked outside of the Banner office in downtown New York City. It was November and not yet too cold as she walked down the street in low-rise black dress pants, black platform heels, and a fitted fuchsia sweater with a two-tone gray and black infinity loop scarf neatly wrapped around her neck. She had her Michael Kors purse on her shoulder and her black leather briefcase in her hand. In case she had time, while waiting for Taylor Barton, she was bringing along some work. They had room in the budget to hire a part-time reporter and Kelsey had wanted to read over the applications that were submitted thus far.

Kelsey ordered a vanilla latte before she slid into a vacant corner booth in the restaurant. She had already eaten a salad for lunch, following deadline, but she wanted to order something while she waited. Waited for this woman named Taylor Barton. A sister to a woman Brady had loved and lost. Again, what did this have to do with her? Kelsey watched the glass door of the Café on the Corner open and close. No one had a look on their face as if to say, *I'm looking for someone I'm supposed to meet here.*

Twenty minutes after one, Kelsey checked her cell phone for any messages from the office. She told Madison she had a meeting and would be back within an hour or so. She was still wondering what she was going to talk to this mystery woman about when the door opened quickly and a woman, about Kelsey's age, in her mid forties, walked in. She was petite, probably only about five feet, two inches, and her blonde hair fell in loose curls onto her shoulders. Her body was in great shape. She was wearing denim leggings and a lime green cable knit sweater. Kelsey could see the toned muscles that formed in her upper arms and legs. This woman was little and cute and looking directly over at Kelsey. And before Kelsey could do anything more than make eye contact, she was standing in front of the booth.

"Kelsey Walker?" Kelsey nodded her head and offered her hand. "Yes, hi, please sit down – unless you want to order something first?" Taylor Barton shook Kelsey's hand and sat down across the table from her after she had placed her Thirty-One tote bag in the booth beside her. "No, I'm fine, thanks. I have to say, I know this seems strange," Taylor said looking as nervous as she must have been feeling.

"It does, yes, so please just tell me why you came to New York. I'm sure you didn't travel just to see me, I mean you're here on business or something else right?" Kelsey asked.

"No. You're the reason for my trip. I am a nurse." Just like her sister, Kelsey thought. "I work at a nursing home, actually, so there isn't any business reason for me to travel." Kelsey remained quiet and waited for more information. "As I told you on the phone, my sister was married to a man named Marty Sutter. Marty was thirty-seven years old when he had to have an emergency appendectomy. He had that surgery at Washington University. My sister – his wife – was a nurse there. And Brady Walker was his doctor. Marty died on the operating table." Kelsey covered her mouth with her hand, before saying, "I'm so sorry, that is awful." Even though it had to have happened more than ten years ago, the story was sad and Kelsey felt the need to express her sympathy to this woman who had lost her brother-in-law. Too soon.

"Thank you, yes, I know. It was a shock to all of us, and a great loss to my sister. Joanie and Marty were trying to get pregnant when he died. We all thought it was just a tragic fluke thing, I mean, really, who dies having their appendix removed?"

"So how did it happen?" Kelsey asked, interrupting like reporters do when they want to get to the meat of the story. She wondered if he had a history of health problems which caused complications during surgery.

"During the surgery, he went into cardiac arrest, and a lack of oxygen to his brain resulted in brain death. I said he died on the operating table because that is really where he lost his life. For two days though, he was kept alive by a ventilator. Then my sister had to accept that he was already gone, and allow the doctor to turn off the machines."

Kelsey swallowed hard, "And Brady was the doctor?" She had not heard that story from Brady before. They didn't talk about his life when he was in Washington, D.C.. Kelsey never had any desire to know about his time with Joanie – and Brady had not volunteered any information. Kelsey hadn't known that Joanie was married when Brady met her. She just knew Brady and Joanie met and fell in love while working at the hospital.

"Yes he was. He was also involved with my sister. Well, it was more like he was infatuated with her. She was married and about to start a family with her husband – but I guess you could say she enjoyed Brady and the attention he gave her, while they worked together. She never cheated on her husband, but she admitted to crushing on Brady. It was nothing more than that though, for Joanie, until after Marty died."

"Taylor, why are you telling me all of this?" Kelsey didn't want to think of Brady as a womanizer. Despite all that had happened in her past with Brady, she always believed he was her soul mate. She knew he acted out of character, and made a crazy decision at Laneview Hospital all those years ago. His choice, in the name of love for her, had cost him *her*. Kelsey left him then, and completely severed their relationship when she uncovered the truth. Kyle had been in a serious car accident which left him comatose. Brady Walker was his doctor, and he and Kelsey began an affair while Kyle remained in a coma and hospitalized for an entire month. Kelsey was torn between waiting for a man she loved to wake up and resume life with her – or to continue to feel the way she had felt with Brady Walker. And be with Brady Walker. They shared an undeniable passion. He made her feel alive, like she had never felt before. Seamless was the feeling. All of those feelings came to an abrupt end when Kelsey discovered Brady was drugging Kyle, medically inducing his coma. He had been buying time. Time to make Kelsey his. And it had almost worked.

Brady's deception and Kelsey's wrath were both in the past now. They had spent more than fifteen years living separate lives and loving other people. Time and destiny brought them back to each other. Their love had created a daughter all those years ago and when that truth was revealed, by Kelsey, the two of them wanted to move forward. Together. They both had chosen to keep secrets, but that was all behind them now. At least that is what Kelsey had believed. And Brady had not given her any reason not to believe that. She believed in him. And in them.

"I found out something, just recently, and I can't stay silent. That is why I'm here today. Finding you and telling you this information is something I need to do, for Joanie. I have to honor her memory. She was my sister." Taylor was tearing up, her pale cheeks flushed, and Kelsey could see the pain in her eyes. Her loss still seemed so fresh, and Kelsey understood all too well. But, something had brought that pain up to the surface again. "At the nursing home, one of my elderly patients was recently dying in my care. He was alone. His wife had died just a year before and they had no children. He was eighty years old and had lived with a secret for the past decade. He said he was never sure about what he saw. But, being on his deathbed he decided to talk about what might have happened, what he actually believed, deep inside of his heart, did happen. This man worked at Washington University Hospital for forty years. He was a custodian. He was on duty, late, the night that Marty was brought into the ER with abdominal pain and had to have emergency surgery. The anesthesiologist had already left the operating room, and soon after, a nurse had walked out. He assumed the patient was in recovery and the operating room was ready to been cleaned. He was prepared to mop the floor, he had his mop in hand, when he opened the side door that led into the operating room. And that is when, he said, he saw the doctor hovering over the patient. The custodian told me he backed away and walked out, without being seen or heard. And later, he learned the news about the man in surgery, dying of cardiac arrest. He heard all of the conversations in the hospital about how sad it was for a thirty-seven-year-old man to lose his life during an operation to simply remove his appendix. He also heard afterward how the doctor had been in love with that man's wife. He didn't want to believe it. He didn't want to tell anyone. He did tell his wife, but she too was uncertain about what he should do. There were times when he came close to just telling the police what he thought he saw, but he gave up when he had found out at the hospital that his favorite nurse, who always spoke to him so kindly, had died of breast cancer. She was the one who lost her husband in that operating room on that dreadful night, and so he thought there was no one left to tell. Little did he know that I, his nurse beside him on his deathbed, am a sister to her."

Kelsey was sitting across from Taylor with her elbows up on top of the table. This was unbelievable. *Who comes up with this crazy stuff? There was no way, just absolutely no way, that Brady could have killed a man. And what the hell does hovering over him even mean?* "There must be some mistake. I don't know what else to say. The man you are speaking of, my husband, is a wonderful doctor. He saves lives for chrissake." *But what about the time he had put Kyle's life at risk? For his own selfish reasons. For love.*

"I felt exactly the same way as you. I loved Brady like a brother. I watched him take care of my sister after Marty was gone. She loved him and she needed him, especially when she was sick – and he was there for her, day and night, until the very end. She died of breast cancer in his arms. I was there, sitting there, beside her bed, as he cradled her and helped her move peacefully out of this life. But what in the world really happened in that operating room that night? Had Brady loved my sister enough to do anything to have her? Did he suffocate Marty to shut off oxygen to his brain and send him into cardiac arrest? Was there even a cardiac arrest? Apparently Brady was the only one in the operating room at the end. Why did the anesthesiologist leave? There are a lot of unanswered questions now. I don't know what to think about Brady Walker. I lost touch with him after he moved back here to New York, but when that man in the nursing home unburdened himself of his secret – to me of all people – I felt compelled to track down Brady Walker. And so I'm here to warn you. I don't think he is the man we all want to believe of him. Nothing good adds up in my mind anymore. He wanted my sister – and he had her, well, for a little while.

The rest of what Taylor Barton said pretty much fell on deaf ears. Kelsey was shaking by the time they parted ways and she made it back to her desk at the newspaper office. "Excuse the old saying Kelsey, but you look like you've seen a ghost." Madison, her secretary, was standing before her in front of her desk. She was holding a few more little pink pieces of paper – with messages on them. Kelsey had not known she walked in.

"I don't feel the best. My meeting took forever and now I think I'm just going to wrap up a few things here and go home." And that is what she did. She drove on the interstate back to her home, a home she shared with her two beautiful children and her husband – a man she loved and needed and desired. She just knew it couldn't be true. *That old man hadn't seen a fucking thing. He had to have been seventy years old at that time and still mopping floors at the hospital. What if he had dementia? Taylor Barton never said what he died from. And poor Taylor Barton. She still missed her sister – and Kelsey's heart went out to her, but honoring Joanie Sutter's memory by telling some crazy story to screw up other people's happy lives was not the way to do it.* Kelsey was done with this. She was done thinking about it.

She didn't have the chance to think any more about it when she arrived at home. Bree was just pulling into her garage as Kelsey was parking her car on her own driveway across the street. She left her purse and briefcase inside of her car and locked it as she walked across the street. It wasn't quite four o'clock yet and Kelsey knew Bree just came from the doctor's office with Sam. She was going to work a half a day and then pick up Sam early from the daycare, for his appointment. She knocked once on the front door, and walked in. It's what they did at each other's houses. They were as close as sisters. *Come on in. My door is always open. For you.*

Kelsey watched Bree carry a sleeping Sam down the hallway, and she stood in the doorway of his bedroom when Bree carefully placed him into his crib. He was a big boy and already had almost outgrown his crib. She covered him up with a light blanket and kept her back toward the door where Kelsey was standing. Kelsey assumed Bree was admiring her sleeping baby boy – but then she turned around with tears streaming down her face. She ran to Kelsey, grabbed her by the arm, pulling her into the hallway and outside of the nursery room door. And that is when she lost it. Kelsey held her close, so tightly, and Bree was holding on to her for dear life. It seemed to Kelsey like the life was draining out of her. She had not seen Bree like that, or felt that kind of intensity in her embrace, since the day her son Max had died.

When Bree had finally stopped crying, the two of them walked into the kitchen with Kelsey's arm locked into Bree's. They sat down on the stools in front of the island and Bree spoke first. "Dr. Michelle thinks that Sam needs some therapy. She wants to start with physical therapy, to get him to sit up independently. Developmental and occupational therapies may follow. And then maybe even some speech therapy, when he gets a little bigger." Bree had not been crying when she spoke this time, but Kelsey had seen in her eyes and on her face – how overwhelmed she was feeling.

"Whoa, slow down, I could see starting with some physical therapy but why plan for all of the others, this early?" Kelsey asked.

"Dr. Michelle is proactive," Bree began to explain, "We may not need any help for Sam after he's taught how to sit, but she is seeing some developmental delays in him which are making her want to act now – and plan ahead."

"So what is the first step?" Kelsey asked, feeling like she needed to remain optimistic and quickly pull Bree from the deep water. This wasn't anything to feel like drowning in. Not yet anyway.

"An Early Intervention Program, apparently every state has them – it's help, therapy, for infants and toddlers who have disabilities or developmental delays. The therapists on staff come to your house, weekly or daily, for as often as the child qualifies. Sam will need an evaluation and we will take it from there."

Just hearing the word *disabilities* pained Kelsey – and she could not begin to imagine how Bree was feeling as a mother. This might not, however, be as serious as it sounds. No one knew for sure. Not yet. And Kelsey wanted to pump some hope into Bree. "Yes, *we* will take it from there. Bree, you are not alone in this. Jack defines the word supportive, Brady is our medical man, and I am the sister you have yet to kick out of your life. I have been and always will be glued to your side, especially when you're going through the crazy shit." Bree smiled and Kelsey took her hand. "Does Dr. Michelle have any idea what could be going on here?"

"It's too early to say, for sure, but anyone with half a brain in our society nowadays knows how to Google for a diagnosis."

"So you plugged in some of Sam's issues…were there any warning signs?" Kelsey asked, "He *is* only six months…"

"There are a lot of syndromes out there, and we live in a world where everything and everyone – if it comes to that – has a label. Sam could have autism." Bree said the word quickly as if she loathed how it felt rolling off of her tongue and she choked on a sob again as Kelsey pulled her close. Brady had mentioned exactly that to Kelsey a few months ago. *Sam could be on the autism spectrum.* Kelsey also had Googled for more information and what she found was a whole different world. There was mild, moderate, severe – and even high functioning forms on what the experts were calling a *spectrum*. If this had to be true, Kelsey found herself choosing to focus on the positives. Kids were diagnosed every day but if they were high functioning, they could sail through life just like everyone else, minus a few quirks. *But who the hell isn't quirky? We all have issues.*

"Hey, hey, hey…come here. Look at me." Kelsey could hear Bree crying in her ear as she held her close. She pulled back out of their embrace with both of her hands on Bree's shoulders and she kept her upright as she looked directly into her teary, red eyes. "One day at a time, remember? We will get Sam through this. He is going to be just fine." Kelsey had hoped, with all of her being, for her own words to be true.

Chapter 7

Kelsey walked back to her house across the street and was retrieving her belongings from inside of her car on the driveway when Brady pulled up alongside of her and parked his car. "You're early tonight," she said to him as he walked around the back of his car to greet her, and she closed her own car door.

"Yes I am," he said, walking up to the front door of their house with her, "I'm looking forward to a quiet dinner with my wife." Once they were inside the house, Kelsey unloaded her purse and briefcase onto a small wooden bench she had placed near the front door for backpacks, purses, or whatever someone was carrying when they walked into the house. "A quiet dinner? In this house? Are you sure you have the right home, Mr. Walker?" Kelsey was teasing him and he spun her around to face him. His hands were on her hips and she, still in her heels, nearly met his height.

"You haven't checked your phone messages," Brady told her, "Bailey and Charlie are staying after school to help organize the silent auction donations and they will be bringing Miles home after his pizza party to celebrate the end of the basketball season." Kelsey walked over to her purse and pulled out her cell phone. "I came home early actually, but I left my purse and my phone in the car because I was in a hurry to walk over to Bree's. She had just pulled in her garage and I wanted to see how Sam's visit with the pediatrician went. Oh, I'm so sorry I missed Bailey's messages. Thank you for taking care of that, honey." Kelsey walked back over to him and stood close and that is when he pulled her into a kiss. These days, he didn't kiss her like that – unless they were together in their private quarters downstairs – because the kids are always around. She kissed him back as he slid both of his hands down to her bottom. When she parted from him, Brady had *that* look in his eyes. There was only one thing on his mind. "I thought your plans were to have a quiet dinner with me," Kelsey teased him, and he took off his jacket and threw it on the chair in the living room. "I think we need to go downstairs and take care of something else first."

She walked down the stairs and into their bedroom, with Brady close on her heels. He was standing there in his scrubs. His shoes and socks were already off, and he was removing his shirt. The sight of him in just his royal blue scrub bottoms, now untied in the front and sitting low on his waist, had still made Kelsey lose her mind. She wanted to put her hands on him. He was watching her from across the room as she took off the scarf she was wearing, then removed her sweater over her head, and finally she slipped off her dress pants. She was now standing barefoot, wearing only her matching lacy pink bra and thong. He was on his feet on one side of their bed, and she stood on the other. He made the first move as he walked around the foot of their bed and stood before her with a look of longing on his face. She smoothed her hands over his chest as he pulled her into a kiss. The two of them shared a passion like neither of them had ever experienced with anyone else. They craved each other. It was intense. It had always been like that, for them, and still is.

Brady kissed her lips, her neck, and then he found her breasts. He had already undone the clasp on her bra as he was making his way down her chest. Her breasts were now free and responding to his touch, his lips, his tongue. The two of them were standing alongside the bed as Brady knelt down on both knees in front of her and slowly slipped off her panties. He found her with his mouth and he wouldn't stop until her hands were gripping tightly on his shoulders and she was calling his name over and over until she came. They ended up on the floor, with Kelsey moving over him. Once again, the two of them so easily found *their* familiar rhythm and got completely lost in the feeling of being together. Like that.

***

"What kind of taco shells do you want, soft or hard?" Brady asked Kelsey as he turned around from the stove where he was separately simmering Spanish rice and refried beans. They had decided on a Mexican dinner, cooked at home, and Kelsey was chopping up the lettuce on the counter next to the stove where Brady was standing.

"I better go with soft since I had my hard fix downstairs a little while ago," Kelsey giggled and Brady slapped her on the behind with his open palm.

"Anytime you need that fix, I'm yours, baby doll." Brady stated, like the confident man he is. He's Kelsey's husband and that fact made him feel like he had the world in his hands. Kelsey was still laughing as she found the sour cream and fresh-mex salsa in the refrigerator. She had not even been thinking about her day's events as the two of them spent some quality time alone – before the kids came home.

"So how did Sam's check-up go?" Brady asked as he walked over to the table to put two plates, forks, and napkins down. Kelsey felt her light mood slowly slipping away as she answered him. "Early Intervention is going to be brought in to evaluate him. Sam definitely needs physical therapy for his trouble with sitting up – and he may need more therapies down the line."

"Is Dr. Michelle thinking about a specific diagnosis already?" Brady did not personally know Dr. Michelle Zahn but he had known she is one of the best pediatricians in New York City. His goal is to get Bailey to work with her before college, before she decides for sure what particular medical field she is interested in pursuing.

"She talked to Bree about the red flags, and she did mention Sam could have autism – although it is too early to be sure yet." Kelsey had tears in her eyes as she said those words. "It's just so hard, you know, so hard to imagine something being wrong with your baby, the child you had planned to love and raise and send out into the world to flourish. I am trying really hard to be what Bree needs right now, but I just don't understand it myself. I don't know how much help I can be to her." Kelsey was now crying and Brady turned off the stove burners and walked over to comfort her.

"You are doing all that you can, right now. We don't know anything for sure – and even if we did, it still doesn't change how much we love Sam. Bree has a great support system, and she's especially damn lucky to have you in her life." Brady was holding Kelsey and rubbing her back when she said, "I'm the damn lucky one. She has been amazing to me, my life support so many times."

***

The two of them had just finished their dinner when Kelsey mentioned the kids arriving home soon. "It's been really nice to spend some time alone tonight, just us," Kelsey said as she looked at her husband sitting next to her at the table. They were both barefoot, wearing lounge pants and t-shirts they had slipped on after being naked together for awhile.

"It is nice. I think we need that once in awhile, more than we realize." Brady looked happy and she had hoped being a family with her and her children made him happy. And then she asked him exactly that. "Brady, is being married to me and being a family with the kids all you hoped it would be?"

"No, it's not." His answer was almost too abrupt and Kelsey momentarily held her breath. "It's better. Sure, it's been a learning experience for me to go from being alone to having a family but I absolutely adore my wife, I cherish how I am getting to know my daughter a little better each day, and I love how it feels to spend guy time with your little man who feels more and more all of the time – like he's also mine." Tears were teetering on Kelsey's eye lashes as she heard her husband describe how much she and her children, their children now, mean to him. "I love you, Brady Walker. So much."

"I love you too, and I would do anything to protect what we have here, with all of us." Brady kissed her on the lips and a few seconds later he stood up to clear the table. And that is when she sat there, thinking. *Absolutely anything? How far would Brady go to keep those he loves intact and close to him? She already knew how far he went with their love when he drugged Kyle all those years ago. Had that been just a one-time-thing when he did something crazy for love? Or was that how he loved? And what else had he done for the sake of love?* She, again, pushed those thoughts out of her mind. She and her husband had just spent an amazing evening together. *He is a good man. It didn't matter what Taylor Barton had said. She is wrong.*

"What are you thinking about over there? You look so serious."

"Oh, just lost in my thoughts, thinking about how happy I am – with you."

"Me too. I've never been happier, babe."

This was her chance. *Just say it. Ask him.* "Not even with Joanie?" Brady turned away from the kitchen counter and looked directly at Kelsey. "With Joanie? Wow, you caught me off guard. You and I don't really talk about our time apart. It's like me asking you specifics about Kyle, I guess. We just don't bring those people up."

"I talk about Kyle with my kids, and I know you've been present and have heard us. We all loved him dearly, and still do. He was such a huge part of our lives. So much like you are to us now," Kelsey explained.

"I understand. He was their father and you loved him just as I had hoped you would love a man – truly and completely – even if it wasn't me." Brady sat back down at the table beside her again.

"I was very happy with Kyle." She hadn't spoken about Kyle, to Brady, in so long. Not, for sure, since they were married. "I still love him and miss him every day. That doesn't change how I feel about you. I have always loved you and now we are making a life together – with Bailey and Miles. We are all very grateful to you for giving us so much of our lives back. It's new and different but so good and such a comfort to have you here, with us."

"I wouldn't want to be anywhere else," Brady said, with so much sincerity in his voice and in his eyes, "The three of you have given me a home, I've never had a real home before. At least not after the first six years of my life. I've literally waited my whole life to feel like this. I know when I walk through the door of this house, someone is going to put a smile on my face and make me feel loved. And I take great pride in being able to give all of that right back – to you and to *our* wonderful kids."

Kelsey was watching him, listening to him, and knowing she needed to ask him. "Do you ever wish you had made a life with someone else? You know, someone like you had found in Joanie – before she died?" Brady's eyes instantly showed a familiar pain. It's the same feeling Kelsey often gets when someone mentions Kyle or when she thinks about him and what might have been – if he had not died.

"I did used to wish, every second of every day, that God had not taken her. We would have gotten married, we would have made babies. After I lost you, I knew I wanted to feel that way again. I knew there was someone out there for me and I wanted to find her and feel whole again."

"What was it like to be with her?"

"I'm sorry, I don't understand your question." Brady appeared uneasy.

"You know, did she make you happy? Did she make you forget…about me?" Kelsey wanted to be the only woman in Brady's heart. She knew she was being selfish, expecting that of him, but he had this incredible way of making her feel like she was – and has always been – his one and only.

"I knew I had to move on, Kelsey. You did, with Kyle, and I was searching for the same," Brady said, "I never stopped thinking about you, loving you, and holding out hope deep inside of my heart for us to one day be back in each other's worlds. And, with Joanie, it was just different. She didn't look anything like you. She didn't act like you. She was unique, she was Joanie, and I loved her. I wanted her in my life forever."

"Brady, I want you to know, I admire you for all you just said. You needed to move on with your life, as I had with mine," Kelsey explained, "We were both happy, apart, and that is okay. It is better than okay now that we have found each other again after suffering so much loss with our other loves leaving us behind. I just wish you could have had more time with her."

"Me too." Brady smiled at Kelsey and touched her hand. "You are amazing, do you know that? I'm honored to call you my wife."

"You're pretty amazing yourself, husband. Can I ask you something else?"

"Anything..."

"Why didn't you marry her sooner? You know, to give her the chance to be a bride, to be your wife, if only for a little while. Every woman dreams of her wedding day. Did she not wish for that?" Kelsey knew that Joanie had died three months before their wedding date. She also knew Taylor Barton told her Joanie was married when Brady met her. Now she was searching for the truth. *Was there any truth to what Taylor Barton spoke of? Would Brady tell her the same story?*

"Joanie was married before. She was married when I met her, actually." There it was. The truth. The start of the truth anyway. Kelsey was beginning to feel like Taylor Barton had it all wrong. About Brady. "Her husband died, very young. He was a patient in the ER one night. I performed the appendectomy. The nurse with me in the operating room had a sick child to get home to. I had just sewn him up so I told her to go on home. The anesthesiologist left as well. I said I could take it from there. Other people had lives outside of the hospital. I did not. I would see the patient into recovery and then go get his wife. I worked with Joanie, we were friends. The very last thing I ever thought I would have to do is go out there into the waiting room and tell her, her husband had suddenly gone into cardiac arrest... and I couldn't save him. I tried. Again. And again. Too much time had gone by, the lack of oxygen to his brain resulted in brain death. He was kept alive for a couple of days on a ventilator. It was heartbreaking to watch Joanie go through that kind of pain. I wanted to be there for her, and I instantly fell in love with her. She needed me, and I needed her – although she probably never knew it – just as much."

Kelsey was wiping away the tears from her eyes. That story was incredibly heartbreaking.

Chapter 8

Kelsey walked through the doors of Laneview Hospital. She hadn't been back there for awhile. That place still had the same feel, for her. So much had happened between those walls – amazing, worrisome, heartbreaking, and life-changing things.

She and her children saw their doctors there, so it wasn't as if Kelsey isn't ever in and out of Laneview. She herself had seen Dr. Judy Winthrop, a wonderful psychiatrist, there for a year following Kyle's death. But, now, Bailey had called her, needing a ride home from her day spent as an intern because Brady was called into an emergency surgery that was going to take several hours. Kelsey texted Bailey as she entered the hospital. *I'm here. Where exactly are you?*

In the lab on floor three. Make a left off the elevator. Second door on the right. Kelsey had felt odd just walking into the lab, but when she did, she found Bailey in there alone. "Hey, why are you in here, all by yourself?"

"I'm just doing busy work, because Brady has not gotten approval yet from the hospital board for me to be present in the operating room," Bailey sighed, "He wanted me to have something to do before you got off of work and picked me up."

"So what exactly is your assignment in here?" Kelsey walked over to look at the computer screen on the desk where Bailey was working.

"To delete files. Every couple of years this hospital throws out the old files of the deceased. Don't ask me why they hang onto the files after people are gone – but they just do. Brady said it is for legal reasons. You know, like in the movies when a body needs to be exhumed to solve a murder mystery." Bailey appeared to be exaggerating and Kelsey giggled at her.

"Tell me what's involved in this deleting process. Can't you just select all files and hit the delete key and call it a day?"

Kelsey asked.

"No, that's the kicker. I have a paper copy for each person, which includes a birth date, death date, and the time frame the person was a patient here. And after I log in their individual code, there are details of surgeries, copies of X-rays, MRIs, and all of that. It's kind of cool to see those scans. So when I retrieve their file on the computer, I have to delete it and then check off and sign off on paper that I found it and deleted it."

"Sounds tedious," Kelsey replied.

"I agree, but I do like to look at some of it and it's work for me to do when I can't be with Brady – although I would love to be watching him performing that brain surgery right now," Bailey's eyes lit up at that mere thought of it.

"Eww, obviously I'm the only one grossed out here," Kelsey said covering her mouth and Bailey laughed out loud. "So are you ready to get out of here and go pick up Miles? With Brady in surgery this evening, I'm thinking the three of us should order take-out."

"I love how you hate to cook, it benefits us kids who like to eat out," Bailey was teasing her mom, "It's a good thing the men in your life have been great cooks."

"Okay, you can stop while you're ahead, missy. I am a good cook – when I have to be." The two of them were giggling and Kelsey felt proud of her teenage daughter. She is already preparing for a career in the medical field while most girls her age are only concerned about their next trip to the mall, or making out with a hot guy.

"I need to go sign out for the day and then grab my backpack from Brady's office." Just as Bailey was going to ask her mom to walk along with her, Kelsey's cell phone rang. "It's Madison at the office, I have to take this," Kelsey said, as Bailey told her just to stay put in the lab for that call, because they frowned upon walking through the hospital halls while talking on cell phones. Bailey quickly left the lab, after saying she would be right back. "Hello Madison, what can I do for you sweets?" Madison, as she often did, was calling to give Kelsey her messages at the end of the day. Kelsey liked to take care of some of her business at home, if it was pertinent, and Madison had given her a few names and phone numbers that seemed important. Kelsey ended that call and she was about to get up from her chair and leave the lab when it dawned on her that Bailey would be going through the names and files of all of the people who had died there in the past couple of years. It had been two years since Kyle's death. He had been pronounced dead at Laneview Hospital. She would see Kyle's name, read his files, and that would break her heart all over again. And, Kelsey was now concerned about Bailey learning the details of Kyle's medically induced coma – orchestrated by Brady. Kelsey had forgiven Brady, and she didn't want to relive it, if Bailey found out. Bailey respected Brady, and Kelsey wanted it to stay that way. Their relationship, although still in the early building stages, is strong and special.

The file on the computer in the lab was still open, and the stack of papers was on the desk in front of her. The names were alphabetized and Bailey was working on the letter L. Newman would be coming up in that pile. Kelsey thought for a moment about thumbing through it. *Maybe she would find and delete it? Maybe she would just read it? Maybe she should get the hell out of there before an employee walked in and caught her and questioned her? How embarrassing would that be? She could also find herself in some serious trouble.* The reporter in her thrived on that feeling of being somewhere she shouldn't be, so she ignored the thought to get up and leave. She is, after all, waiting for her daughter to come back. And her husband is the chief of staff of the hospital. She could talk her way out of it – if someone walks in.

Kelsey looked through the papers quickly. As she was searching through the M's, she noticed each name had a numerical code, and she remembered Bailey saying a code was required to log in to a file.

Newman, Kyle P. It had come up in her hands quicker than she had expected. Or maybe Kelsey just wasn't ready to see his name and feel how she always felt when she opens a drawer at home and finds his expired driver's license, or his police badge, or their wedding picture. Or his two-tone gold and silver wedding band that she had worn on a box chain around her neck for months following his death.

She spun around in her chair to face the computer, ML99BC was the code she punched in. There wasn't a picture ID, just information. She began to read his health history. He had had mandatory, yearly checkups with his physician after he moved to New York City, from Pennsylvania, and was hired by the New York Police Department. His month-long stay in the hospital, following the car accident, was documented there. Kelsey read it all closely. And then she reread it. There was nothing there about the thiopental drug. The drug she had remembered finding out about when she snooped in Brady's office all those years ago after becoming suspicious about Kyle actually having been medically induced into a coma. By Brady. It was all true and Brady had admitted to being the doctor who administered the drug, repeatedly, to keep Kyle under. Kelsey found it a little odd how some of Kyle's information – which had once been in his medical files – is now gone. It was something Brady was ashamed of, she knew, but why delete it? What if something had come up in Kyle's life following his recovery that would have made doctors question possible side effects from being given thiopental for so long? Again, that was pertinent information, Kelsey had thought. She continued reading and found regular doctor check-ups throughout the rest of Kyle's life. He had not been hospitalized again after his accident. The final page of his records did show the details of that dreadful day when he was found slumped over the steering wheel of his car – and the autopsy results had revealed how he suffered from a brain aneurysm. She would never forget that day when she had to identify her husband's body – in the morgue. *So painful. So unreal. Why was she making herself relive all of this?*

She was about to close out of the file, she decided not to be the one to delete it. It just didn't seem right to *delete* him.

He already had been *deleted* from her life, something that was completely out of her control, and she didn't want to be the one to hit that key. It was too final. She didn't want Bailey to have to do it either. The information about Kyle's medically induced coma was not there, so maybe she shouldn't worry about Bailey seeing the file and having to delete it. Kelsey thought about just preparing Bailey, telling her Kyle's file would be in there, to delete, the next time she is back working in the lab. She was wondering what was keeping Bailey as she was about to click out of the Kyle's file and move away from the computer. And that's when she thought about that day.

The day she and Kyle came to the hospital for his follow-up exam after his accident and dreadful coma. She had not wanted to see Brady again. Their affair was over, and it had been a bitter end once Kelsey discovered Brady's deceit. Kyle, however, had been having reoccurring headaches and Kelsey knew she needed to be there, with him, when he talked to his doctor. Dr. Brady Walker. That was the day Brady had ordered one final scan for Kyle, just to make sure all was well inside of his head – she remembered Brady saying – especially since he was still suffering from the headaches. She remembered the month, day, and year. She remembered having just accepted Kyle's marriage proposal.

Kelsey scrolled back up and through the information on the computer monitor. There was the accident, the coma, the month-long hospital stay. And then there was his yearly physical, carbon copied for the NYPD, one year later. *What about the follow-up scan?* There was no record of it. Kelsey wanted to see the X-ray copy. She didn't know why, she had just wanted to. Since Kyle had died, she often wondered if the car accident and head injury had resulted in his untimely death – from a brain aneurysm. *What did it matter now? She didn't know how to read a medical X-ray. And it wouldn't change anything or change how it had happened.* She just wanted to see the information. Again, it was the reporter in her, she thought. Bailey had said if a patient had any scans done, it would be there. *Why wasn't it all there for Kyle?* No details about his medically induced coma – and now no record of his final scan at Laneview Hospital. *This was strange.*

Kelsey heard someone coming down the hallway so she clicked out of Kyle's file on the computer, and put the stack of papers back on the desk – just as Bailey entered the lab. "Sorry I took so long, mom. I'm ready if you are. I spoke to the anesthesiologist who walked out of the operating room for a few minutes and he said Brady is going to be here late, probably another three or four hours for the surgery alone."

Kelsey followed Bailey out of the lab. This was going to bother her – and weigh on her mind for awhile. *Why had some of Kyle's files been missing?*

Chapter 9

Kelsey rolled over in bed and heard the shower water running. She opened her eyes and saw the bathroom door, off of their bedroom, closed and there was light shining from the bottom of it. Brady was home from the hospital. The digital alarm clock on the nightstand beside the bed showed it was a few minutes after eleven. Kelsey had only been asleep for an hour. She was actually surprised she had been able to fall asleep so quickly, considering the questions running through her mind.

A few minutes later, Brady slipped into bed beside her. His hair was wet, his skin was still damp from the shower, and he was wearing a pair of boxer shorts. Kelsey slept in lacy boyshorts and a sports bra. In her forties, she had read about how women who wore a bra to bed kept their breasts perkier as they age. Kelsey found a comfortable sports bra brand, called Barely On, which she religiously had worn to bed now for a few years. She liked the feel of the sheets against her bare skin, so sleeping in only underwear easily became her preference. When sleeping next to Brady, however, it didn't matter what she was wearing. She could wear flannel pajamas buttoned up to the neck and they would be coming off – with Brady's hands on her.

She turned to face him in the dark as he covered up with the sheets and duvet. "Hey there…you're awake."

"Yeah, long day for you?" she asked, moving closer to him.

"Yes, but that's the way it goes sometimes," he said, touching her face, the side of her cheek with his fingertips. "Thanks for coming to pick up Bailey. I don't like it when emergency surgeries interfere with her internship days with me."

"She understands. I was in the lab with her for a little while. She said she had some busy work, deleting files, to do in there."

"Yes, very boring for her, I'm sure."

"I actually found it interesting when I was thumbing through the paper files and found Kyle's information." She had just come right out and said it, and she also was going to ask him about the missing details.

"What?" he asked, "Oh, gosh, I'm sorry I didn't even think about that. Was Bailey upset?"

"No, I was the one who found it. I was in the lab alone when she left for a few minutes. It occurred to me how Bailey would see Kyle's file and I either wanted to delete it myself or prepare her for it."

"Kelsey, you are not authorized to be on the hospital's computer – much else to delete any files," Brady actually giggled when he spoke to her, "You are a piece of work with that reporter mind of yours. You think you can just waltz in anywhere and check things out." Brady was still laughing at her and she was smiling in the dark. It is true, she developed that frame of mind over the years. She wanted to figure things out, and sometimes she caught herself pushing hard to get to the base of every story. She is that kind of an editor too, often returning the written stories to her reporters and telling them to ask more questions. She wanted more information. She wanted the complete story.

"So what are you gonna do to me, doctor? Turn me in to the hospital board?" Brady pulled her toward him with a force that instantly created desire between the two of them. "Do you wanna be beat?" he was teasing, and, Kelsey answered, "maybe," before they kissed.

"I didn't delete the file and I didn't tell Bailey that she may have to," Kelsey still wanted to talk about this.

"You know, anyone who deletes anything on that computer has to initial it – even Bailey. So you can't be touching any of that. Seriously Kelsey, you're going to get my ass fired." Brady was exaggerating about losing his job, but he did have concerns about raising eyebrows with the board of directors. It had taken him quite some time to convince them to allow his daughter to work beside him as an intern. The board supported Brady's work with the high school career program, but they questioned whether or not it was a good idea to have his daughter working beside him. They wanted a professional environment inside of Laneview Hospital. Brady agreed with them and had thought to himself, at the time, *you should have been around seventeen years ago when I met the woman of my dreams and made love to her under this roof – and on the rooftop.*

"I'm sorry, I will behave myself," Kelsey apologized with a sassy tone in her voice, "It's not like I marched in there on a mission. It just happened, and I was curious, so I looked. With that said, I'm hoping you can explain something to me..."

"Sure, what?" Brady was still touching her as he had propped himself up on one elbow, faced her, and listened. "The thiopental information was missing. There was no record of Kyle being medically induced into that coma. And, the scan – the last scan you ordered for him the day I was there...

when we said goodbye for the last time – also was not there."

"Really? I can't imagine why anything would be missing from anyone's files," Brady answered, abruptly. "Are you sure? It had to be there. There really isn't any explanation for why it wouldn't be."

"I thought maybe you didn't want the drug-induced coma information on record." Kelsey was being very careful how she chose her words right now. This was not a subject she wanted to rehash, and she knew Brady was ashamed.

"I made that choice so long ago. And yes, in part, it was something crazy that I did for love," Brady began to explain, "but, what you have to understand is exactly what I told you back then and that is, as a doctor, I made the right decision for Kyle. His brain needed rest in order to heal. What I should not have done was keep that decision from you. You should have known what I was doing. I was just afraid you would think I was doing it only for love, for your love."

This was difficult for Kelsey to discuss. Even after all of these years, even after his death, she still felt protective of Kyle. Protecting *him* was the main reason why she had walked away from her relationship with Brady. "We've moved beyond all of that, Brady. And then, today, when I opened Kyle's file and found some information missing – I don't know, I just felt like I had caught you covering up your tracks."

"I wouldn't do that because there was nothing to cover up – at least not medically. Look, I'm still sorry I lied to you."

Brady reached for her hand and she held his.

"I know, and now I just don't want Bailey to stumble upon any of that information. But there was more missing than just the continuous thiopental dosages," Kelsey pressed. "I told you, the Cat Scan, which Kyle had done just a week or so after he was released from his extended hospital stay, also was missing."

"Maybe you overlooked it? It really doesn't matter though, babe. I don't mean to be harsh, but why would we need any of that information now? That scan was clear. I read the results myself that day, and then I sent Kyle on his way – and he moved on with the rest of his life. With you." It still pained Brady to remember that day when he watched the two of them walk out of the hospital. Together. Kelsey wasn't his anymore – and he had spent the next fifteen years missing her. And still wanting her in *his* life.

"I know, and you're right, it really doesn't matter what is or isn't in that file now. I guess my main concern now is Bailey not having to be the one to see Kyle's name and information – and press the delete key. I know it seems trivial, but it's emotional for us. Still."

" Of course it is," Brady agreed, "How about if I take care of it? Before Bailey returns to the hospital for her internship again next week, I will delete it."

"Thank you for being here to make life easier for me – and for the kids."

"You know I would do anything for all of you." Brady held her close, and soon they both had fallen asleep. Content in each other's arms.

Chapter 10

Bailey and Brady were walking through the hospital halls and when they passed the lab, she asked him, "So was it you who deleted my dad's medical file?" Brady looked at her, surprised, but with kindness in his eyes. He didn't want to see her in pain and he knew losing the man she loved as her father was painful and life-changing for her. It was painful for him too, to hear her call him *her dad*. Still. Even after they both now knew the truth. Brady is her biological father. And he wanted to be *her dad*.

"Yes. To be honest, I had not thought about Kyle's file being in there when I gave you the assignment. Your mom came across it the day she was here to pick you up. You know how curious she is and, well, she helped herself to the computer in the lab and found it. It upset her, and rightfully so, and she just didn't want to bring you that kind of sadness. And neither did I." By now the two of them had reached a patient-room door and Brady took the chart out of the wall compartment and began flipping through it. She admired him. He is a good doctor. He is teaching her so much about medicine, years before she will begin to study it in college. She loved him for so many reasons. And she knew, now, he was protecting her. Like a father.

"Thanks Brady," Bailey said, "even though I would have been just as curious to take a look at some of the scans after the car accident, it still would have hurt to delete him."

"That's exactly what your mother said. And you're welcome. Now let's get to work." Brady opened the patient-room door for her and she walked in ahead of him. What she didn't know is there were no digital copies of any scans in Kyle's file. Not anymore. There hadn't been for years. All of the CAT Scans following the accident were deleted. Years ago. Especially the one where there appeared to be a bulge or ballooning in a blood vessel in the brain. It had not shown up at first. On the final scan, however, it was visible and had looked like a berry hanging on a stem. It was a brain aneurysm which didn't rupture until fifteen years later. And apparently it created no health problems, just reoccurring headaches. A symptom. A warning sign. An indicator that something could be wrong. When the aneurysm did rupture, it took Kyle's life.

***

Kelsey was thinking about Kyle as she sat at her desk, in her office. She had a framed photograph of him, with her kids, sitting on her desktop. She had taken the photo of the three of them while they were on vacation, the summer before Kyle's death. On the beach in Destin, Florida in the white sand on a beautiful hot and sunny day. The boys were barefoot in the sand, wearing khaki shorts which ended at the knee, and long-sleeved white button-down shirts rolled up to their elbows. And Bailey was wearing a lacy white tank dress, her hair was down, well past her shoulders. They were all suntanned and happy and Kelsey was lost in the memory as she stared at that beautiful photograph. It was one of her favorites. And such a treasure to her now. Next to that picture in a silver frame was another, this one of Brady and Kelsey on their wedding day. It was a full-length vertical photograph of them. Kelsey looked stunning in an ivory, off-one-shoulder, full-length, silk dress with a side slit revealing almost her entire leg. And Brady was wearing a tan suit and a blue tie. That tie, chosen by Kelsey, had matched his bright crystal blue eyes. She loves him. And she loves her new life. She is happy again. They are happy again. Her children are doing well and Kelsey smiled to herself as she glanced at their picture again. And then her thoughts were interrupted by Madison on the speaker of her desk phone. "Kelsey, you have a call on line one, Taylor Barton."

Kelsey froze. Not again. Not this woman with her crazy accusations, and lies. Kelsey momentarily thought about not taking the call. She didn't need this in her life. But then she picked up the phone, brought it to her ear, and pushed her finger on button number one. "This is Kelsey Walker."

"Kelsey, it's Taylor Barton again. He left a note."

She wanted to say *Who?* and *What are you talking about?* but she knew Taylor was speaking of the older man who died. The older man who thought he saw something in the hospital the night Taylor Barton's brother-in-law died. "Look, Taylor, I don't mean to be rude, but I'm super busy right now and I just don't have time to listen to any more of this."

"You need to hear it. You need to know the man you're married to is not the person you think he is," Taylor persisted, "I know how you are feeling because I felt the same way, but now I have to honor my sister's memory and uncover the truth."

"Would your sister really want you acting like this? Come on, Taylor, you're dredging up the past to cause pain and it's unwarranted. And I want you to leave me, and my family, alone!" Kelsey hung up the phone. She disconnected the call. She was done with Taylor Barton. And she later instructed Madison not to put that woman's call through to her again. Madison didn't ask any questions, she just assumed Kelsey didn't want to run with her story idea for the newspaper. Kelsey certainly didn't want to run with Taylor Barton's story.

She wanted to put that phone call, from her, out of her mind. She wasn't going to go there. *Who cares if the old man left a note? Hadn't he already caused enough confusion on his deathbed?* Kelsey truly felt sorry for Taylor Barton. She needed to move on. Her grief was obviously still consuming her. It happened to people, Kelsey thought. It had almost happened to her. And to her kids. But now, more than two years later, they were making it. And Brady was a very big part of the reason why.

Kelsey may have given up, but Taylor Barton had not. From her home in Washington, D.C., she searched on her computer for Laneview Hospital in New York City. She clicked on the staff icon. And then, more specifically, the chief of staff. His picture was there, online. As was his physician's office phone number.

Chapter 11

Kelsey was honking the horn on Bree's driveway. She knew she was saying goodbye to Jack and to Sam, but *alright already, let's go!* It was no one's birthday or anniversary or any special occasion at all. It was just going to be an overnight girl's trip for Kelsey and Bree. Kelsey came up with the idea and talked to Jack about it. He agreed, Bree needed a break. He even, generously, booked and prepaid for their reservations at a bed and breakfast in a historic townhouse, just one hour away.

When Bree stumbled out of the house with her overnight bag in hand, looking back and waving to Jack holding Sam at the front door, Kelsey knew she had to get that girl out of there. It was written all over her teary face, she was having second thoughts. Kelsey got out of her car, grabbed Bree's bag, and placed it in the trunk. "Come on, it's okay, he will be fine. Thank you so much, Jack, see you tomorrow," Kelsey yelled as she blew Sam a kiss from the driveway. Sam was happily flapping his hands in his daddy's arms and Kelsey pointed out his good spirits to Bree as they backed out of the driveway.

"He is in such a good mood this morning. So why isn't that making it any easier to do this? To leave!" Bree looked torn. She wanted to spend some time with Kelsey, she knew she needed a break from playing the mommy role to a high-maintenance baby, but she hated to leave him.

"Stop, would you rather have him crying and screaming? No, you wouldn't, because then we wouldn't be going on this mini road trip and God knows we both need this sister!" Kelsey squeezed Bree's knee, pressed her foot down harder on the gas pedal, and drove out of their neighborhood.

***

The two of them were giggling as they unlocked the door to their room at the bed and breakfast. "The front desk clerk thinks were gay," Bree said, laughing, as Kelsey closed the door behind them. "And who can blame the guy?" Kelsey asked, "We hang all over each other like a couple of glorious weirdos and now we just rented a room with a king-sized bed for the night!" The two of them were howling with laughter. Neither one of them cared what anyone else thought. They are friends who have a damn good time together. They have been through thick and thin together and counting on each other through it all is a given. They love each other so much. Unconditionally. The support gained from that kind of friendship, that kind of sisterhood, is matchless and should be treasured. And it is.

It was only noontime and they had nothing on their agenda. The two of them settled into their room in the townhouse and then left awhile later for some lunch at a beautiful outside café Kelsey had read about online. When the two of them were seated at their table, they ordered soup and salad, and their first bottle of wine.

After the waiter left with their second empty wine bottle, Kelsey suggested they browse through the little shops nearby and then stop at a local market for some more wine to take back to their room at the townhouse. They were giggly, but not yet too loopy as they left, did a little shopping, and returned to their room a few hours later.

They were sitting at a patio table on the balcony outside of their room, splitting another bottle of wine. The October air temperature was in the sixties and the two of them were comfortable wearing jeans and long-sleeved shirts and flip flops. They had each gotten a pedicure just a few hours earlier, after lunch and in-between their shopping. Kelsey's toes were painted neon pink, and Bree's were sky blue.

"You know if you get me drunk, I won't have to think about how much I miss my baby," Bree admitted. She had been quiet the past half hour and Kelsey noticed her texting outside when she was getting a bottle of wine and two glasses from inside of their room.

"I know you miss Sam. Have you checked in with Jack to see how he's doing?"

"He's having a good day," Bree sighed, and tried to smile, "And yes I do miss him, but more than anything I just worry something will happen to him when I'm not there. I mean, I know Jack can handle him and his tantrums but sometimes he bangs his head or throws himself back when we try to help him sit and I just want to be there to protect him from getting hurt, or worse."

"That's a natural mom feeling. We all want to protect our kids. I don't think Sam will hurt himself. I've seen him look startled when he has landed too hard, back onto the floor behind him. He stops and realizes what he's done and I believe he knows it hurts." Kelsey has gotten used to seeing Sam's quirky, stimulated behaviors, but she also knew a red flag is a red flag. His recent gains in physical therapy, however, had given all of them a little more hope. Sam, at nine months old, could now sit up independently. The therapist, through the Early Intervention Program, continues to meet with Sam three times a week for one hour sessions at his daycare center. Bree purposely scheduled his therapy around her client schedule at work and she always made sure she was present during Sam's therapy sessions to observe and learn from the therapists. Three hours a week of therapy is not going to fix any child if a parent is not willing to learn the trade and the tricks and work with a child at home to meet the goals. Bree had almost quit her job over the idea of not being with Sam, all day long, to work with him. To help him. Both Jack and Kelsey had told her not to make such a drastic decision about her career. To give it time.

Sam would come around. It was Kelsey who finally convinced Bree not to quit. First, she told her it was so important for any baby to be around other little ones. They learn from each other and especially because Sam has delays, she shouldn't shelter him. Bree agreed and then Kelsey told her something else to convince her not to give up her job. A job that had grown into a career and a sizeable salary for Bree. *You never know what can happen in any relationship. You and Jack, I know, are in this for the long haul, but if something were to happen to him – or even if he would walk out – you would be left untied to both the father of your son and an income to live on and support yourself and your son. Look at me, look how quickly Kyle left this world and left his family. Plan ahead for survival, Bree. I'm so grateful for no money problems. After Kyle died, I at least knew my kids and I would be okay financially because I have my job and Kyle was a wise investor for most of his adult life.* Bree took Kelsey's advice and continued to send Sam to daycare. He had good days and bad days while staying there, and the phone calls to Bree – when Sam was having a meltdown – stopped. Jack, unbeknownst to Bree, went to the daycare center and spoke with the director, asking her to not allow her employees to call Bree at work when they were about to dial crazy just because Sam is a bear to take care of. It was their job to handle him, and unless he was sick or they had a serious concern, aside from the ordinary Sam issues, he asked for Bree to be left alone. She has a job to do, and she needs some peace of mind throughout her work day in order to do it. And Jack knew how badly Bree wanted to be involved in every second of every day of Sam's life. He also knew time away from him is good for her. And not knowing about every scream or cry or unsettled moment is even better for her. The daycare did give Bree a written report at the end of every day, but somehow reading about a rough moment or even a rough couple of hours is easier to digest – after the fact, after it is over and done with. Bree was feeling better about getting away as she finished another glass of wine and set it down on the glass tabletop. "Kel… thank you."

"For what?" she asked splitting the last of the wine left in the bottle between their two glasses. "For this. This mini getaway has already helped me clear my head and recharge. I know when I walk back into my house tomorrow, I will feel refreshed and ready to tackle Sam again. No matter what lies ahead."

Kelsey squeezed her hand, resting on the tabletop. "You do not have to thank me. You have been my rock so many, oh hell I've lost count of how many times, and this is not something I am going out of my way to do for you. You mean the world to me and your baby does, too. Sam will prevail. He may not be the boy you envisioned raising. You may have to alter your expectations a bit, but he's yours. He brings us all so much joy with his contagious smile and hilarious belly laugh. He's a keeper."

Bree had tears in her eyes. "Yes he is, and you're so incredibly right about all of that. I can do this."

The two of them had originally planned to dress up and go out for a nice dinner, but too much wine and the relaxed feeling of not having anywhere they had to be changed their minds. And their plans. They decided to walk down the street, less than a mile, to eat cheeseburgers and potato-skinned fries. The burger restaurant was advertised on a flyer at the front desk when they checked into the townhouse and they had both commented on how good a juicy cheeseburger with the works had sounded. Sometimes, they strayed from their healthy eating habits and this trip was one of those times.

Two bites into her burger, Kelsey looked up from the booth where she and Bree were seated and she focused on a woman walking through the restaurant. She was with a man who was a head taller than her. She was a short but fit woman, probably in her forties, and she reminded Kelsey of someone. When the woman turned her head and looked up at the man she was with, Kelsey breathed a sigh of relief now knowing it wasn't her. Besides, the odds of it actually being her were slim. She lived in Washington, D.C.. The woman had just *looked like* Taylor Barton. That is all Kelsey would have needed. She was done with that woman. And she had hoped she would never call her again. *Give up, already. My husband is not the man you say he is.*

"Hello? What the fuck? Who are you staring at and why do you have that look on your face?" Bree was dipping a gigantic potato fry into some ketchup and wondering what, or who, so suddenly had changed Kelsey's mood.

"Oh, nothing or, I mean, no one, I just thought I recognized that woman over there for a moment. But, it's not her." Kelsey took a big bite of her cheeseburger and began chewing. She wanted to get back into the moment of enjoying good food and time alone with Bree.

"Well whoever you thought she was, poor her. The look on your face was new to me. I thought you liked everybody? Kelsey, the dreamer of world peace, has finally found someone to dislike? I have to hear this story," Bree was teasing but Kelsey knew that was partly true. She didn't like Taylor Barton. She didn't like her because she is a liar. And looking to stir up trouble where there isn't any.

"I thought she was someone who called me at the paper about a month ago. She wanted to meet, I did, and it was a waste of my time," Kelsey began to explain.

"For a story idea?" Bree asked.

"No, to dredge up the past," Kelsey answered, and Bree took her napkin and wiped her mouth and her fingers with it. "The woman's name is Taylor Barton and she is a sister to Joanie, Brady's former fiancé who died of breast cancer before they were ever married."

"Why would her sister contact you? Does she live in New York?"

"No. She lives in D.C. and traveled to see me." Kelsey had not told Bree, or anyone, this story. She wanted to erase it from her memory. It wasn't even worth talking about. "She made some accusations against Brady, from all those years ago when he lived and worked at Washington University Hospital."

"What kind of accusations?"

"She said Brady manipulated his relationship with Joanie. He had fallen for her while she was married," Kelsey continued to explain.

"She was married?" Bree asked. "I don't remember you saying that?"

"I didn't know. Taylor told me that Brady wanted Joanie, and Joanie enjoyed the attention and the flirting at work. She said Joanie and her husband Marty were rock solid and trying to have a baby. Then one night Marty must have had some pain that landed him into the emergency room with an appendicitis attack. He had to have emergency surgery, Brady was the surgeon on his case... and he died on the table."

Bree gasped, she didn't intend to, but she did. "What? Oh my God, what the hell happened?"

"I know, so sad, he was only like thirty-seven years old," Kelsey explained, "Apparently he went into cardiac arrest just as the surgery was completed and the lack of oxygen to his brain caused brain death. He was put on a respirator and then taken off a few days later. There was just no life there." Kelsey didn't even know Marty Sutter, but she felt sad telling his story. Sad for the man who died young. Just as her husband had. She still could not wrap her mind around Kyle only having forty-three years of life. It just was not fair. To him. To her. Nor to their children.

"That is awful. So Joanie was a widow who ended up engaged to Brady, but she also died…the story is sadder than we knew, huh?" Bree stated, "So how is that supposed to be Brady manipulating his relationship with this nurse who became a widow? He obviously cared about her and was there for her when she was grieving. I could see exactly how their relationship formed."

"Taylor said just as much," Kelsey said, "Brady was there for Joanie, pulling her through her grief, and she fell in love with him. Apparently Taylor really liked Brady and was so grateful to him for the way he was there for her sister especially while she was sick and then later dying from breast cancer. He was a knight in shining armor in her eyes."

"And now?" Bree asked.

"Now, she, who also is a nurse and works in a nursing home, claims that an old man confessed something to her on his deathbed. He didn't know she was a sister to Joanie, but he told her he had witnessed something – or thought he had – working at Washington University years back. He told her he thought he saw the doctor, alone in the operating room with Marty Sutter, hovering over him and he wondered the rest of his life if that doctor had caused Marty's death."

"What? As in kill a patient who happened to be the husband of a nurse he was crushin' on? Commit murder so he could have Joanie?" Bree was piecing together what she thought Kelsey was saying.

"It's unimaginable. Brady would not do something like that. I mean, come on, what did the old fucker see? He was eighty years old when he died. And this incident supposedly happened a little more than ten years ago. He could have been half cray cray then." Kelsey didn't mean to demean his suffering or any disease he may have had, but it pissed her off to think one old man was putting a lie into people's minds from the grave.

Any other time, Bree would have giggled at Kelsey's word choices, but now the topic was too serious. And the idea of it being true was scaring her. Taylor Barton and some old man were making assumptions and accusations about her best friend's husband. They were a family, all of them, and this seemed absurd. "Tell me more about the old man, and how was he even present in the hospital to see anything?" Bree inquired.

"Apparently he worked on the cleaning crew there for most of his life. He was working that night and must have thought the operating room was empty and ready to be sanitized. The operating room nurse and the anesthesiologist were both already gone for the night. Brady was taking over in recovery, because he said everyone else had lives to get home to. He offered to stay and get Marty into recovery and then go get his wife in the waiting room."

"So you talked to Brady about this? You asked questions?

And he knows about this Taylor lady's crazy accusations?" Bree felt better knowing Kelsey had gotten to the truth, from her husband.

"Yes and no," Kelsey said, "I did ask Brady some questions about his life with Joanie and he told me the same story of how she was married before, and her husband died. I did not tell him about Taylor Barton contacting me and what she has all said."

"Why not? I think he should know what Taylor is up to! I think he should know this woman tracked you down to share lies," Bree now understood why Kelsey did not like a woman she hardly knew, but thought she saw a few minutes ago in the restaurant.

"I don't know why. I just felt like keeping the peace. He and I have dealt with all of the lies we've had between us. I forgave him years ago for prolonging Kyle's coma, and he forgave me for keeping Bailey's paternity a secret after all this time. We are finally moving on. We are happy," Kelsey sighed.

"Is a part of you afraid it could be true? Bree asked, putting some pieces together, "There is a similarity here with Brady and how he drugged Kyle, induced his coma, in order to pursue you."

"Do you have to play Sherlock Holmes here? I have thought about how freaked out I was with the possibility of Kyle being in danger at Brady's hand. I mean, that is the reason why I ended our relationship. I didn't trust Brady, and I was afraid of how it appeared he was hurting another human being in order to benefit himself. But, I no longer see it that way. I think I did at first, but not for very long. And now, I sure as hell do not believe Brady could have murdered Marty Sutter. He saves lives. He is a good man." Kelsey did not want this trip to turn so serious. The two of them were supposed to be having fun. Enjoying some girl time.

"I don't believe it either," Bree admitted, "I love Brady, he's family to me. I know how much you love and need him. This is just bizarre. So the conversation you had with Taylor Barton was a month ago and you just told her off and she traveled back to D.C. with her tail tucked between her legs?"

"It appeared that way – until she called my office again last week," Kelsey rolled her eyes, "She had one thing to tell me, and after she said it, I told her to leave me and my family alone. And then I told Madison I would not accept a call from Taylor Barton ever again."

"What did she want to talk about the second time?" Bree asked as the waiter interrupted them to take away their empty plates.

"She said the old man left a note, I don't know, I guess in his will. And then I hung up on her." Kelsey didn't care then and she still didn't care now. *Fuck the note. Whatever it said.*

"You, the curious reporter I've known my entire life, didn't ask any more questions?" Bree, herself, wanted to know what the hell was written in that note to make Taylor Barton call again.

"It doesn't matter to me. I could have driven like a bat out of hell to get home to Brady that day. I could have told him what that old man and the woman who almost became his sister-in-law were thinking and saying about him. But I didn't," Kelsey said, "because I don't believe any of it is the truth."

"So what did you do?" Bree asked, "I mean, really, when I was married to Nic – bless his heart, the son of a bitch – I always confronted him. And believe me, it felt like there was always something to confront him about."

Kelsey recalled what she did. She walked into the house with Brady, which happened to be empty and kid-free for a few hours, and the two of them were consumed in passion. She had thought about bringing up Taylor Barton to him, while they were alone without the kids' ears in their conversation, but instead she chose to be intimate with him. "I did ask him about his life with Joanie, I brought it up subtly and asked him if he was happy with her. He's always saying how happy he is with me, and the kids, and I just threw it out there. I asked him if he was happy with her, with Joanie. And then the conversation unfolded from there and he told me the truth. I mean, his story compared with Taylor's. He was in the operating room alone. He was heartbroken to tell a devastated wife in the waiting room that her husband had a complication during surgery and she now had to make the heart-wrenching decision to say goodbye to him because life support was the only thing keeping him on this earth."

"So that's it? You're moving forward, never caring what the note said?" Bree was still not convinced Kelsey should walk away from this.

"Yes, exactly. That old man knew he didn't have a case. I mean, seriously, hovering over? I'm not going to let a dead man or a grieving sister affect my happiness. And if you must know, as soon as I saw my husband that very same day I didn't second guess him, I made love to him. I love him and I do trust him. He has given me no reason not to. The past is in the past."

Bree laughed out loud, "You two act like you did when you met all those years ago. You can't keep your hands off each other or your bodies separated for very long. You do know that I've never seen you like this with anyone? Back then, when Brady Walker first came into your life, and again now, you are wildly addicted to that man."

Kelsey smiled at her dearest friend, "And that's never going to change. The charge I get from my wild addiction, as you put it, is going to be life-long. I want to spend the rest of my life feeling loved unconditionally, seeing my children adore this man, and having orgasms with him until I'm old and wrinkled." They both laughed out loud together. It was time to lighten the mood and end this conversation. The past was in the past.

Chapter 12

Kelsey and Bree both returned from their overnight trip feeling rejuvenated and happy to have found some time to catch up again. Bree went home and fell back into her routine of dealing with Sam and making a life with Jack. That man is a gem. There is a stress in his life he's never known before but, together, with the woman he loves, he is determined to see them all through it.

Across the street, Kelsey was catching up with her children as soon as she walked in the door and set her overnight bag down. Bailey and Miles were talking about everything they did at home and they repeatedly mentioned Charlie.

"Hey, guys, slow down with your stories. Wasn't Brady here yesterday and last night with you two?" She assumed he was at the hospital now, but he had told her he cleared his schedule to spend time, while she was away, with the kids. Kelsey did not leave her kids alone overnight, ever, and having Brady a part of the family now allowed her to plan a mini getaway with Bree. Or so she had thought.

"No, he was at the hospital after lunch yesterday and all night long," Bailey said, "and he's still not back." Kelsey was surprised. She heard from him late last night. He texted her to wish her goodnight and told her he loved her. She responded with the same, but never asked him about the kids because she also had texted a sweet message to Bailey for her and Miles. It never occurred to her that her kids were alone. No one told her.

"Oh my goodness, so you two were here, alone, all night?" Kelsey wanted to get upset but she realized being married to a doctor is something she is going to have to get used to. You can make plans, but it may not always go the way you intended.

"Charlie stayed with us. Brady gave us permission, so all three of us had a sleepover in the downstairs living room. In fact, Charlie is not a morning person so he's still down there, sleeping," Bailey laughed, and Kelsey was okay with that. She knew Charlie is *a friend* to Bailey and she also felt grateful to have a strong young man in the house overnight with her kids.

***

And when Brady finally did walk into the house an hour later, Kelsey was making brunch for everyone. She had an egg casserole with hash browns, cheese, and bulk pork sausage baking in the oven and she was readying a platter of fresh fruit. The kids were hungry because all they had eaten last night for dinner was junk food. She was about to tell her kids to go downstairs and wake up Charlie, when Brady came home.

"Hey babe, you're back. I thought I would beat you home." Brady was wearing dark-washed jeans, a burnt orange long-sleeved polo shirt, and brown loafers. He always came home from the hospital wearing scrubs, unless he had a meeting with the hospital board

"I am. Bree needed to get home to Sam," Kelsey said, kissing him after he leaned toward her and she sliced the green stem off of a strawberry with a sharp knife. "So the kids said you had an all-night emergency? Dressed like that?"

"Yes, two emergency surgeries, and I took a shower at the hospital and changed because I had a board meeting first thing this morning. It's been crazy and I'm glad to be home. How about you? I missed you. Did you two ladies behave yourselves?" Brady winked at her and she noticed the dimple on his left cheek. His smile sent tingles through her body.

"Of course not...why behave?" she teased him, "We had a good time, catching up with no interruptions. No sleep though...and probably a little bit too much wine." Kelsey was smiling at her husband and he was thinking how beautiful she looks. And having her as his wife now is a dream come true. "I hope you're hungry, because I am about to call the kids in here to eat."

"Yes, I am. I just need to run downstairs to file some paperwork in my office. Be right back," Brady said grabbing his briefcase off the floor which he had brought inside the house with him.

Downstairs, it was dark and Brady walked straight through the basement and into his office, never noticing Charlie was asleep on the couch. He flipped on the light in his office, set his briefcase down on the desk, and opened it. With that, his cell phone rang and he retrieved it from the back pocket of his jeans.

"This is Brady Walker," he answered, and listened before speaking again, "Yes, I would say life support for a day or so, for the family to be able to say goodbye and all. Okay, sure, keep me updated." Brady ended the call and then added, aloud and alone in his office, *"Good riddance, Taylor Barton. You got what you deserved."*

And that is when Brady left his office and went back upstairs to be with his family. What he didn't know is, he was not alone in the basement. And his phone call had not been private. Charlie Thompson was lying very still on the couch, covered up to his chin, wide awake. He had heard every word. The tone in Brady's voice had surprised him. He knew Brady as a gentle man. And now he was a little scared. *Who is Taylor Barton? And what happened to her?*

***

Charlie was the last person to come to the table in the kitchen. He was wearing his jeans and t-shirt from the day before and those clothes were wrinkled. He had splashed some water on his face in the downstairs bathroom next to the living room and then brushed his teeth with a travel-sized toothbrush that he sometimes carried with him. He had looked into the mirror and saw the puzzlement on his own face. *Should he tell Bailey what he heard? Or maybe Mrs. W. should hear it from him? Maybe it was nothing at all and he should just forget it? And not tell anyone.* When Charlie sat down at the table, Bailey teased him about sleeping the day away and he gave her a sweet smile as Kelsey thought he seemed uncomfortable. That wasn't Charlie. Not in their house anyway. He was present so often that he was like part of the family.

***

Kelsey was still in the kitchen when everyone else had scattered after they had eaten. Bailey walked Charlie outside to his car when he said he needed to get back home. He and his mom were spending the day together. He had outgrown so many pairs of his jeans in the last month and his mom wanted to take him shopping and spend some time together.

Kelsey still wished one of these days she would run into Blair Thompson again. It was unreal how their lives had intertwined again, now through their children. Brady and Miles were outside playing basketball on the driveway and Kelsey smiled at them through the window in the kitchen. Just as she was about to leave the kitchen to go downstairs and check out the sleepover mess left behind in the living room, she heard a cell phone ringing on the counter. It was Brady's and she noticed Laneview Hospital was calling. She picked it up, as she had many times before, to take a message for him. He didn't always keep his cell phone in his pocket when at home. He mentioned to Kelsey before how when he's present with his family, other people can wait. This is his job, however, and Kelsey knew the hospital could never wait.

"Kelsey, honey, how are you?" It was Mary Sue, the head nurse at Laneview Hospital. After three decades, the hospital is a second home to her. She loved her job at Laneview and Kelsey knew she loved Brady like a son. They are dear friends and Kelsey thought a lot of her as well. She is supportive of Brady and obviously adores him. And now, most likely, Kelsey had thought, Mary Sue was calling with an emergency that would send her husband back to work today.

"I'm doing well, thank you Mary Sue, how are you?" Kelsey asked her, smiling.

"I'm wonderful dear, but I do need to be the party pooper and interrupt your day with that handsome hubby of yours. Tell him he's had enough time off yesterday and this morning and now we need him to fill in for Dr. Flanagan in the ER." Kelsey was not sure if she heard her right. *Time off? Had he not been working nonstop at the hospital until he walked through the door this morning?* "Um, I'm sorry, he just got home from being there all night... I thought."

"Oh, no, he said he was spending some time with the family – with the kids, I believe." Mary Sue was quick to correct her.

"Right, I was out of town for a day and I just assumed Brady had gotten called in to the hospital. He and I need to get caught up again, that's all," Kelsey was feeling panicked inside. Where had he been all night long and this morning before he returned to their home and lied to her? "So do you need him to come in right now?"

"As soon as he can, yes," Mary Sue answered, "Could you tell him that, dear?"

Kelsey walked outside, feeling overwhelmed with questions, when Brady turned to her and flashed his charming smile. "Hey babe, did you come out here to join us?" Miles had the look on his face as if to say, *gee not a girl*, but he knew his mom could hold her own in basketball. He actually liked playing with her.

"The hospital called. You need to go in and sub in the ER," Kelsey couldn't look at him very long, she turned away from him and began walking back into the house. And he followed her after he told Miles he was *sorry*, but he *had to go* and they would *play later*. Kelsey let the kitchen door close behind her, and a few seconds later, Brady opened it.

"I'm sorry I have to go back to the hospital. I will call you to let you know how long I'll be. Maybe we can have a nice dinner tonight? Just the two of us?" He walked toward her and Kelsey turned to face him. He put his hands on her shoulders and pulled her close. And then he kissed her. She couldn't resist him. But it was there. The doubt. The wonder. The mistrust. It was surfacing and, this time, Kelsey was not going to let it go. Not until she had answers.

***

Brady was on his way to the hospital when Kelsey walked through the living room and saw Charlie, through the window, making his way up to the front door. She met him at the door and opened it. "Charlie? You're back? I thought today was your shopping trip with your mom?" Kelsey stepped back to welcome him inside. He looked forlorn as he walked past her and sat down on the couch. He was so used to making himself at home there, and because he cared so much about all of them – this was going to be especially difficult for him. Charlie had talked to his mom and she encouraged him to tell the truth. He decided it would be better to speak to Mrs. W. first, because he didn't want to worry Bailey. It could be nothing. But he trusted Mrs. W. to make that call. If she heard what he came to say, maybe she would tell him what he overheard was nothing to worry about?

"Charlie, if you're here for Bailey she just left to get a mani-pedi with Emily. Remember? She mentioned those plans at brunch." Charlie nodded his head, and Kelsey sat beside him on the couch. She put her hand on top of his, which was resting on his knee. "Are you okay? Is your mom okay? You know I'm here for you, right? You can talk to me about anything, honey." Kelsey wondered if Charlie was struggling with his sexuality. Maybe he is having relationship trouble? Maybe he is still getting used to that truth about himself? Maybe he isn't entirely comfortable in his own skin yet? Kelsey was suddenly worried about him. She loves that boy as much as Bailey does. And she knew he had come into their lives for a reason.

"I am fine, my mom is fine, too. I know Bailey isn't here. I came back to talk to you." Kelsey kept silent and allowed Charlie to continue speaking. He seemed to be struggling with finding the right words. "I was asleep downstairs in the living room this morning when Dr. W. came down and went into his office. He was talking on his cell phone...and I overheard him say something... and I'm not sure how to tell you this." Kelsey felt her heart rate speed up. *What in the hell is happening?* First, Mary Sue, on the phone, indirectly brought to light the fact that Brady had lied to her, and now Charlie is so obviously disturbed by something he overheard Brady saying. "Just tell me, Charlie. It's okay, I want to know what you heard."

"Um, okay, it wasn't much, but I heard Dr. W. say life support would be good for a day or so, until the family said goodbye. And I didn't think anything of that. I mean, he is a doctor and it sounded like he was discussing a patient with another medical person. Then, I heard him say he wanted to be kept updated and he ended the call." Kelsey was suddenly feeling relieved. *That was it? That is what Charlie was so worried about? That was nothing.* And then Charlie spoke again. "Then, Dr. W. spoke aloud to himself, 'good riddance, you got what you deserved.'" Charlie looked at Kelsey, his eyes were wide and hers were puzzled. "Who did? Who got what they deserved? Did Brady say a name?"

"Yes he did. Taylor Barton," Charlie answered her.

Kelsey felt the color completely drain from her face. Thank God she was sitting down because she knew her legs would not have been able to hold her up at this moment. Her knees were weak. Taylor Barton was somehow back in the picture again. And Brady was involved. "Mrs. W., are you okay? You don't look so great. Do you know who Taylor Barton is? Is this something I should not have repeated?"

Kelsey immediately pulled herself together. Charlie may have been eighteen and officially on his way to becoming a man but he still was a kid in so many ways. Inside of his tall frame, broad shoulders and muscles with moderate definition built up in the school weight room, he was still a boy. And this boy was worried he had said something wrong. "No, I am glad you told me this, Charlie. I will get to the bottom of it, okay? I'm sure it's nothing. And I want you to not worry about what you overheard. I do want you to keep this between us though, okay? Don't mention it to Bailey until I find out more information. I don't want to worry her over nothing." Charlie nodded his head in agreement, he had already mentioned to his mother how he overheard something and needed to speak to Bailey's mother. He couldn't shake the feeling of urgency, about it. He hadn't given his mother any specifics because he loved Bailey and her family and he didn't want her to try to protect him from them by telling him to keep his distance. She couldn't keep him from them – and he didn't think she would try to. Not unless there is a solid reason. And he hoped there isn't. He did know what he said had bothered Mrs. W. far more than she admitted to him.

It had most definitely affected Kelsey, because when Charlie left, she walked down the basement stairs en route to Brady's office. A part of her wanted to barrel down the stairs as fast as she possibly could. But, physically, she couldn't. It was as if her feet were heavy and hardened like cement. She was in slow motion, trying to put one foot in front of the other. She was on her way to finding out more. And she wasn't so sure she wanted to get there as fast as she could. She wasn't in a hurry to feel her world unravel.

Just as she thought, he had left his briefcase behind. He never took his briefcase with him to the hospital, unless he had a board meeting. And Kelsey thought he had one this morning. That is, after all, what he told her. And she, of course, had believed him. He has never given her a reason not to believe him, not since he has been back in her life and married to her for a year. The lies were behind them. Or so she had thought.

Kelsey carefully opened his briefcase. She felt like an intruder. This is her husband's office. And she is snooping for information. Information she, again, was not so sure she wanted to find. But she did find it. And the fallout was about to begin.

Kelsey was staring at an airline ticket stub. Proof that Brady had gone out of town yesterday afternoon and returned this morning. He had flown roundtrip to Washington D.C.

Chapter 13

There had been nothing more in his briefcase. Nothing more to tell Kelsey why in the world her husband secretly traveled to Washington D.C. for such a quick trip. But, Kelsey knew – thanks to Charlie – it had everything to do with Taylor Barton.

She closed his briefcase and left the ticket inside, just as Brady had left it, and she made her way into their bedroom, downstairs. She sat down on their bed and her mind was reeling. She was sitting on *their* bed. She was sharing a bed with this man. She was sharing a life with this man. Her husband. He is the father of her firstborn, and he is playing the role of *dad*, so flawlessly, to both of her children. Did she know this man at all? Was she putting herself and her children in danger? This is Brady, for chrissake. It seemed inconceivable. It had to be. Because at this very moment, Kelsey could not fathom dealing with more pain. Hadn't they all been through enough? Why was this happening to their newfound contentment? And happiness. *They are happy.*

Suddenly, Kelsey's thoughts flashed to Kyle. They too were happy. And then it all fell apart. He died and her world spiraled out of control. And that world, as she had known it with Kyle, was gone forever. She pulled herself from that downward spiral with the help of those who love her – and with Brady's love. He came back into her life and saved her, in so many ways, from drowning. She needed to talk about this, so she did. To Kyle.

She sat alone, downstairs in the bedroom she shared with her new husband, and she spoke aloud to the husband she had lost. *Hey you, up there, it's me bothering you again. What is going on? Please give me some guidance here. You know what is happening, I know you're watching over us. Lead me to the truth, Kyle Newman. Give me a sign that I'm doing the right thing here. Work with me. Keep me strong if there is something I need to know. For myself. And for our kids. I love you. And suddenly I'm really missing the simplicity, the normalcy of the life we had together. Help me…please.*

Just as Kelsey stopped talking to Kyle, up in heaven, the door to her bedroom flew open. She was startled but then calmed herself as soon as she saw Miles. He ran to her and threw himself into her arms. "Mom! Mom! Please hold me! Please hold me!" Kelsey enveloped him inside of her arms and held him as tight and as close as she possibly could. She could feel his little heart beating against her chest. "What honey? What is it, are you okay?" She pulled him out of her arms so she could see his face.

"Mom, I know you are not going to believe me but I just saw dad! Oh my God, mom, I just saw daddy!" Tears were streaming down his face as fast as the words were coming from his mouth. And Kelsey's mouth was hanging wide open. She *did* believe him.

"You what? Tell me! Right now! What are you talking about?" Kelsey could now feel her own heart about to beat out of her chest. She pulled Miles down onto the bed, beside her, and he spoke about his surreal experience.

"I was outside, shooting hoops, and I couldn't get a three-pointer to save my life. I can always get it, but not today. I was feeling bad about not being good anymore. I have to be good. For dad. He thought I was good and he was teaching me how to be better. That is when I looked up at the sky and I yelled, 'Come on, daddy, be with me! I need you!' I closed my eyes before I tried again, one last time, to make that shot. I was ready to give up. I hate basketball when I can't be good. Good, like daddy wants me to be." Kelsey was allowing Miles to speak. His story was taking awhile, but she was patient as he told her more. "And then I saw him. He didn't look like an angel. He looked like himself, like my daddy. He was standing under the basket, where he always stood when he told me to shoot from farther away. He was wearing his favorite Saturday blue jeans, with the holes in the knees, and a gray POLICE t-shirt, you know, the ones Bailey likes to wear." Kelsey was wiping away tears streaming down her face. It was her turn to cry. "I heard what he said mom. It was so clear. It was *his* voice."

"Miles, what did he say? Word for word, please tell me. I will believe you." With those words said, Kelsey truly could not believe this was happening. Miles didn't seem as frightened as he continued to speak of his surreal experience outside on the driveway.

"He said, '*you can do this and so can your mom. I love you, your sister, and your mom and I'm always with you, all of you. Don't ever forget that.*'" Miles was crying hard again, he was so moved. "And mom," he said choking on his sobs, "I made the shot for him. I made it! He helped me and I wanted to thank him, I wanted to run to him and feel him hold me again... but then he was gone. Oh God, mom, please help me bring him back. Please, I miss him so much!" Miles was sobbing so hard and so loud that Kelsey couldn't take it. She cried equally as hard, right along with him. She cried for her son's pain. She cried for their loss. Kyle was never coming back to them. He was, however, still so very present in all of their lives. And he had given her the sign she had asked him for. *You can do this and so can your mom.*

Chapter 14

Miles was so overwhelmed with the experience of seeing Kyle that he had fallen asleep on her bed after crying in her arms. Kelsey laid him down, covered him, and went into living room area downstairs and logged on to the Internet. She did a search for Washington University Hospital in D.C. and found a phone number. She then went upstairs to retrieve her cell phone, from where she left it in the kitchen. She had to make that call.

She asked for admissions and waited to be connected. "Hello, this is Angela Haag, I am calling from Laneview Hospital in New York City. Our chief of staff, Dr. Brady Walker, would like an update on the condition of Mrs. Taylor Barton." She was taking a chance. Was Taylor even a patient in the hospital? Did she even have *a condition*? Kelsey had hoped to God, she did not.

"Yes ma'am, you can tell Dr. Walker that she was unfortunately removed from life support thirty minutes ago. It's incredibly sad. The same thing happened to her brother-in-law years ago in this hospital. And, please, Angela, tell Dr. Walker it was so nice to have him back in our facility last night." The person on the phone obviously was chatty, revealing way too much information to a total stranger who had just lied about who she is and where she is calling from. And that person on the other end of the phone at Washington University Hospital also had known Brady – and just saw him, last night. Kelsey thanked the woman for the information and ended the call. *What in God's name had happened last night? And what did Brady know about it?*

At that very same moment, Brady also received the news. He was on the rooftop of Laneview Hospital, fighting the unclear connection on his cell phone. Dr. Reiss, his friend and former colleague, called to tell him the news. Taylor Barton is dead.

Brady heard enough. He also ended his call to Washington University. Standing on the rooftop, as the wind blew on his face and through his short dark hair, he remembered last night's events. He had flown to D.C. when he heard Taylor Barton was having a scheduled gall bladder surgery. Dr. Reiss had told him she would be going under for a standard laparoscopic procedure. By chance, Brady had found out Taylor was going to have surgery. He was on the phone, just a few days before, talking to his friend, and Dr. Reiss happened to mention the sister of Joanie Sutter. He knew Brady loved Joanie and her family, so he casually mentioned that fact. And when Brady heard the news, he knew what he had to do.

Taylor Barton had been calling him for a week. Every day. She told him she had already met with his wife, a month ago, and was ignored. She also told him about the elderly man on his deathbed and how she now believed, after more than a decade, Brady had killed her brother-in-law. Taylor hadn't held back. She told Brady he was done. He was caught. And he was going to pay. Unless he paid her a half a million dollars. She was leaving her husband, wanting to start a new life with her three children. She was tired of the nursing home, and fed up with death and dying all around her. Watching her sister lose her husband and then her own life had done her in. She had spiraled out of control. She also told Brady too much. And it was going to cost her. Her life.

When he boarded the flight to D.C., he had a one milliliter syringe full of thiopental. He was going to meet Dr. Reiss at the hospital. They had made dinner plans, because Brady told him he would only be in town for one evening. Dr. Reiss had also agreed to allow Brady to stand in during Taylor Barton's surgery. After all, the two of them were practically family. Once upon a time.

Brady used his old badge from Washington University Hospital to slide and unlock the entrance door in the back of the building for staff use only. It still worked. He still had access. He was wearing his scrubs, with the syringe in his pant pocket. Taylor's gall bladder had been successfully removed. The anesthesiologist said she wouldn't be awake and coherent for awhile and he stepped out for a brief moment. He had a terrible addiction to cigarettes and he would just be a few minutes, after he had a smoke. Dr. Reiss was left in the operating room with Brady. The two of them were talking as Dr. Reiss walked over to the waste bin to remove his bloody surgical gloves, and then with his back to Brady he walked over to the sink to wash his hands. And Brady knew, all too well, when Elliot Reiss washed his hands following any surgical procedure, he scrubbed and rinsed, and scrubbed and rinsed some more. It used to annoy Brady to no end. *For chrissakes Elliot, wash your damn hands and move on!* But, right then, Brady needed that time. Just enough time to remove the syringe from his pocket and inject the entire dosage of thiopental into the IV connected to Taylor Barton. And that is exactly what he did, quickly, while continuing to discuss an unbelievable play during a recent NBA game.

The syringe was back inside of Brady's pocket, empty, when Dr. Reiss finally turned around to find his patient entering cardiac arrest. Both doctors sprang into action. They tried. And they tried again. But it was too late. And Brady knew it would be too late. But he worked as if he had really been striving to save the woman who had threatened to rock his world. He was not going to lose Kelsey. Not again. Not ever.

Taylor Barton was as good as dead. She had suffered from cardiac arrest, and a lack of oxygen to the brain resulted in brain death.

Brady is a skilled physician. He does extensive research on all of the drugs he administers. He knows anesthesia medications, like thiopental, can be frighteningly dangerous if used improperly. When a patient is given too much anesthesia, an unusual drop in the heart rate or breathing will immediately occur. If the patient cannot pass through the initial complications from the anesthesia overdose, they will suddenly hit a threshold after which they will crash and stop breathing entirely. At that point, cardiac arrest, oxygen deprivation, and brain damage are often inevitable. And again, Brady knew that. All too well. Because the same thing had happened to Marty Sutter, in that operating room.

With Marty, however, it had been Brady's first time administering an overdose of thiopental. So he was terribly nervous. His hands were shaking, and he had dropped the syringe onto Marty's chest and it rolled over to the opposite side of the surgical table and landed next to his ear. Brady immediately leaned over him, his chest pressing hard on Marty's face as he lay there unconscious. Brady stretched a bit further to retrieve the syringe quickly, before someone came back into the operating room. And that is when the custodian had seen him, from the side door behind him... hovering over the patient.

***

Kelsey was sitting on the couch, drinking her third, full glass of wine when Brady came home. It was late, half past midnight, but she couldn't sleep. The kids had both been asleep for a couple hours and she was just sitting there thinking, and drinking to take the edge off. She knew she had to say something to him. She also knew she needed to be very careful. She wanted to get to the truth without confrontation. She was planning to get a few answers from him, then investigate further. On her own.

"Oh, hi babe, what are you still doing up?" Brady set his cell phone and keys down on the table by the door and walked over to sit down beside her on the couch. God how he loved coming home to her. She is his world.

"Waiting for you, and having a little wine to unwind from the day." And, *oh my*, what a day it had been. *What is this man, her husband, hiding from her?*

"I'm glad you waited up for me, I've missed you the past couple of days," he said, taking the wine glass from her and tipping back a considerable amount of it into his mouth before he swallowed. And then he kissed her. Hard and aggressively on the mouth. And she responded. She always responded.

"Hey… can we talk about something?" she asked him, half out of breath.

"Of course. What's on your mind, Mrs. Walker?" Yes she certainly is Mrs. Walker. She had taken his name one year ago, already. She was happy and honored and fulfilled being his wife. But, now, there were so many questions and doubts and fears running through her mind.

"I should have told you something…weeks ago. But, I didn't want to upset you or worry you. I thought it was crazy, I thought *she* was crazy, so I let it go." Before she continued, Brady interrupted. "You thought who was crazy?"

"Taylor Barton."

Brady's eyes widened. "Joanie's sister. She contacted you, didn't she?" he asked, and Kelsey was surprised by his words, but she went along with him, calmly and carefully.

"Yes, twice in the last month. First, she traveled here, to New York, just to see me, and then just last week she called me again. Did you know this? Have you talked to her, too?"

"She has been hounding me and yes she told me that she contacted you and met with you," Brady confessed. "I'm sorry you've had to put up with her, as you said, craziness. And you are exactly right, she is crazy. I never harmed Marty Sutter. I wouldn't kill a man. And I never would have put Joanie through that kind of pain. Taylor is bananas."

"That's what I thought too." Kelsey would have believed him. Any day. If she hadn't heard Charlie's confession, if she hadn't found out from Mary Sue how Brady didn't work all weekend, and if she hadn't discovered the plane ticket stub.

"Good. Believe that, babe. Taylor has not been the same since Joanie died. Most recently, she planned to leave her husband, take their kids, and leave Washington, D.C." Kelsey was surprised Brady knew so much so she inquired how. "She told you all of that?"

"Yes, and she tried to blackmail me for a half a million dollars," he admitted.

"What?" Kelsey asked, surprised. Was Taylor really that insane? Before she died. And will Brady tell her she did, in fact, just die?

"She said there was proof, a note left behind from a deceased hospital custodian – the one she told you about – but I found out she made it all up. There was no note," Brady explained, "She was just trying to freak me out and get some money. Enough money for her to start a very comfortable new life."

"Why would she even think she *could* freak you out? Is there something you are not telling me?" This was her chance and she took it. Kelsey wanted to know if Brady had ever done anything to make Taylor think she could blackmail him.

"No, you know as much as I do. She was crazy. You do need to know… Taylor is dead. She died on the operating table at Washington University last night," Brady's voice was calm and quiet. Kelsey feigned surprised, "Oh my God… what happened to her?"

"She went in for a routine gall bladder surgery. The procedure was done laparoscopic and all seemed well – until she went into cardiac arrest," Brady explained, "She couldn't be saved. Elliot Reiss was the surgeon. He did everything he could. They put her on a respirator so the family could say goodbye and try to get some closure."

"That is insane, Brady. That is Marty Sutter's story all over again! What the hell happened to her and her brother-in-law? How do you explain that?" Kelsey wanted to hear exactly that. How was *he* going to explain that? And what did *he* have to do with it?

"I can't explain it. It's just sad that it can happen. Anytime we put a patient under, there is a risk. And, please, do not take this the wrong way…but a part of me is a little relieved to hear she is out of our lives. She didn't have anything on me, but she was stirring up trouble and the way she contacted you is just weird."

"I agree, this has all been a little too weird," Kelsey said, looking at him, and then he told her he needed to get in the shower and he would see her downstairs shortly. She stood up, to walk through the living room to turn off the lights after Brady had gone down the stairs, and that is when she heard a voice from upstairs. Bailey had been sitting on the top step the entire time.

"Mom, what is going on?" Kelsey was startled and wondered how much her daughter, *their daughter*, had heard.

"I'm not sure what you mean, honey," Kelsey said to her as Bailey descended the stairs and stood in front of her mother.

"Charlie told me. I knew something was bothering him and I made him tell me. I'm scared, mom. I can tell you are, too. You also are digging for information. Do you think Brady told you the truth just now?" Bailey was whispering in fear of being overheard, and Kelsey knew it was time to talk about this. She had kept it inside long enough.

"No, I do not think he is telling me the truth. Bailey, I need you to be strong and help me get to the bottom of this. I found out Brady flew to Washington, D.C. this weekend. That is where he rushed off to while I was gone overnight, with Bree. And Taylor Barton just died. The same way her brother-in-law died more than ten years ago. Brady is keeping something from us."

Bailey felt so scared at this moment, but the last thing she wanted to do was allow her mother to see her fear because she knew how much she needed her help right now. And what she was thinking and piecing together in her mind had scared her the most. "Mom, did you hear what Brady said to you? I don't know if it's because I am studying with him and wanting to understand all about medicine, but I read between the lines when he said something just now…"

"What did he say? What did I miss?" Kelsey was impressed by her daughter's perception and intelligence. She had worked side by side with Brady for months and it was possible that she better understood how he thinks in a medical environment.

"Let me do some research before we draw any serious conclusions, but his words are ringing in my ears right now. He said, *'anytime we put a patient under, there is a risk.'* I think there is a connection there, for Marty and now Taylor."

"Bailey, that is brilliant. You think this is anesthesia related?"

"Yes…I'm thinking it's pentobarbital or thiopental."

Kelsey's heart could have easily stopped at that moment. *Oh dear Lord. Not again.* Was thiopental the culprit? Had Brady continued to use that drug to his advantage? For his benefit? Had he used it for murder? Not once, but twice? Bailey's theory made more sense than she realized. She had not known about Brady's history with thiopental and how he used that same drug to keep her father in a coma for far too long. Yes, *her father.* Kyle Newman was Bailey's father. And right now Kelsey was beginning to regret bringing Brady Walker back into all of their lives.

Chapter 15

It was a typical weekday morning in their house, and Kelsey was grateful for how well Bailey was able to pull off acting like nothing was wrong when Brady was around them, in and out of the kitchen and living room, before he left for work. She had told her, last night, to not let on she is suspicious. It had become quite obvious to them Brady could talk his way out of absolutely anything – and this time they wanted to remain one step ahead of him. Bailey was allowed to talk about this with Charlie, but no one else could know. Kelsey stressed to Bailey for Charlie to keep this between the three of them. He should not tell his mother, or anyone, what he overheard and how it has led them on a search to uncover the truth.

Before she left for school, Bailey pulled her mother aside when Miles was not within earshot. "Mom, I know you didn't have a chance to last night, because Brady was with you downstairs, but I did a search on my laptop up in my bedroom. An overdose of thiopental can be deadly. The patient will get to a point where they stop breathing entirely, and the end results are cardiac arrest, oxygen deprivation, and brain damage. Mom, do you really think Brady killed two people that way? Do you really think the man who we know and love – the man whose blood I have running through my veins – could do that?" Bailey felt sick to her stomach, she was awake most of the night, thinking and wondering what will happen to their family – and to the man who, by blood, is her father.

"I don't want to believe it, baby girl," Kelsey said, pulling her daughter close. "Believe me, I wish we weren't even thinking it could be true. But, if it is, we need to know. And he needs to be stopped."

***

Kelsey knew she had to figure out her next move. And fast. Taylor Barton's body was in the morgue – and before she was embalmed and buried, or maybe even cremated, Kelsey needed some proof of how she died.

So that is when she decided to call Washington University and track down Dr. Elliot Reiss. When she heard his voice on the other end of the phone, she knew the angle she was going to take to reach this man. He sounded forlorn. He sounded detached. And Kelsey knew why. Brady had told her enough about his friend for her to know he is a man of great compassion. He was in charge when a woman in her forties died over the weekend on his operating table. There was no explanation for her sudden cardiac arrest and that fact was driving him to the brink of insanity. He had seen the reaction of her husband and her three teenage children, in the waiting room, when he had to tell them Taylor Barton – a wife, a mother – was brain dead and only being kept alive, minute to minute, on a respirator. A machine they would have no choice but to pull the plug from. The memory of that moment – their faces, their tears, their screams, their shock, and their grief – was eating him alive. He lost patients before, but never like this. Never unexplained.

"Elliot, it's Kelsey Walker. Brady told me what happened. How are you?" Kelsey had only met this man one time, but she liked him. And she knew he liked her, too. He loved Brady like a brother so he had open arms for his wife. And Kelsey appreciated that far more now than he realized.

"Oh, hi, Kelsey, it's sweet of you to check on me. I'm a goddamn mess. I can't explain this, I'll never be able to explain this. I mean, I know I couldn't save her…we both tried. Had Brady not been present in the operating room with me and had he not tried just as damn hard with me to save her, I would be even worse off right now." There it was. She now knew, for sure, Brady had something to do with Taylor's death. Something or everything. *God help her, she was about to find out.*

"Maybe there is something you can do…" It was a suggestion and maybe a long shot to try to keep this a secret from Brady, but Kelsey had to make an attempt to convince Elliot to do it. Now. "Do an autopsy. Find out if there was an overdose of thiopental. Don't ask questions, Elliot, please, just do this. You will get peace of mind, and we will get answers."

"What are you saying? Who would have overdosed her?" Elliot was scared, but this all suddenly began to make sense to him. Brady was coming into town for one night only. Brady had insisted on being present in the operating room. Elliot merely thought Brady cared about the woman who almost became family to him.

"I am saying do this and do it now, before funeral arrangements are made," Kelsey could not believe she was in cahoots with another doctor to bring down her own husband. "And Elliot, do not tell Brady this. I mean it. I swear to God, all of this will blow up in our faces if you breathe a word of this to him."

"Kelsey? Is Brady not the man we believe him to be?" Elliot felt the shock waves ripple through his body. *Could it be true? Was his patient indeed murdered? By his friend and former colleague?*

"I don't know, Elliot. I sure as hell hope I'm wrong about this, but I think Taylor's death was intentional, at Brady's hand. Please, just hurry and do this. Get some answers."

***

And so he did. Elliot Reiss knew the pathologist well at Washington University and he asked him to do this favor for him, and to be discreet about it, before the body was moved from the morgue to the funeral home. He was present throughout the autopsy and had asked the pathologist to cut right to the chase. Do not check out anything else. Check for a thiopental overdose. He did, and both doctors had an answer. Taylor Barton was murdered. Right under Elliot's nose. He trusted Brady, loved Brady like a brother, and when he called Kelsey back on her cell phone later that same day, he had said as much to her.

"I understand, Elliot," she said to him, but what she really wanted to say was… *Tell me about it. How do you think I feel? This is the man whom I pledged my love and my life to. He is my world now and I am responsible for bringing him into my children's lives.* Kelsey ended their call after asking him to keep this between them, for now. She had more things to uncover. She was digging for *why* Brady did this. She was uncertain what her next measure of action was going to be, but she never said as much to Elliot. She only said she would take it from here, and he had responded, *"Make him pay."*

Chapter 16

Kelsey was sitting in Bree's living room, in a comfortable recliner chair. She had her legs crossed so Bree wouldn't see how badly her knees were shaking. She made it through the day at the newspaper but she didn't know how – because her mind was constantly on Brady, what was happening, and all she had uncovered thus far.

Bree was tending to Sam, who was sitting on the floor chewing on his favorite blanket while watching on old episode of The Brady Bunch on the TV. When she did step away from him, she sat down on the couch just as Jack was walking through the front door, wearing his workout clothes and carrying both his gym bag and briefcase. His unannounced entrance set Sam off. He threw himself back onto the floor and started wailing and knocking on the sides of his head with the knuckles on both of his hands. Bree immediately jumped up and went to him, on the floor. "Hey, hey, don't hit. Don't hit yourself," Bree emphasized. "It's okay. It's just daddy. He is home from work. You're okay…" Bree managed to calm Sam and Jack kept his distance for a few minutes. "Geez, Jack, I didn't hear you pull up. Usually a warning that someone is here helps Sam to cope a little better when he sees them," Bree was looking at Kelsey now, and she responded, "He did great when I came in. Probably helped that I brought a pack of fruit snacks I knew he would want, and somehow that sort of makes him want me here." Kelsey was smiling and Jack told her she is a smart woman. But, as Bree was watching her, she could tell something was not quite right with Kelsey. She needed to get her alone. To talk.

"Hey Jack, I know you just came from the gym so why don't you shower before dinner…and take Sam in there with you," Bree suggested, "You know how he loves the water."

"Sure will. Come here buddy," Jack said, picking Sam up off of the floor. Sam hadn't been listening to where he was going so he was thrown off again and immediately hit Jack in the face. "Whoa buddy, no hitting. Let's go get in the water."

Jack held Sam's hand down as he carried him out of the room.

"Okay Kel, let's hear it. What is bothering you?"

Kelsey could hardly keep the panic out of her voice when she replied, "Taylor Barton is dead." Bree's face dropped. "She's what? What the fuck happened to her? She's like our age, right?"

"She was in her forties, yes. She had gall bladder surgery and died on the operating table. She went into cardiac arrest, was put on life support after being declared brain dead, and then her family was forced to pull the plug. Her poor husband and three teenage kids…" Kelsey's voice trailed off.

"What? That sounds like the same way that Marty guy died, her brother-in-law, right?"

"Yes, exactly the same way. This is a long story, Bree, and I don't know how much time you have, or myself for that matter – because everyone is going to be getting home across the street here soon – but I have to tell you this. And you are not going to believe it," Kelsey felt so panicked each time she thought about it, and now saying it out loud flipped her out even more. "When we left town for twenty-four hours, so did my husband. He flew round-trip to Washington, D.C. to assist with Taylor Barton's surgery. It's the same pattern, Bree – with both Marty and with Taylor. She was hounding him, threatening him, and tried to blackmail him. He told me about her death, but he does not know that I found out he was there. He told the kids he was working an emergency all night."

"Come on, Kel, you don't think he killed her, do you? You told me you didn't believe he had anything to do with Marty's death either! What the hell changed your mind?"

"Charlie."

"Bailey's friend?"

"Yes, he spent the night with the kids when I was gone, when Brady slipped out of town. Charlie was asleep on the couch downstairs in the living room the next morning when Brady came home. He overhead him on the phone. Brady did not know Charlie was there. A colleague of his was informing him of Taylor being about to be removed from life support. After he ended that call, Charlie overheard him say *'Good riddance, Taylor Barton. You got what you deserved.'*"

"Kel, what are going to do? If he is doing this, he has to be stopped, but you have to be careful. Oh my God, get out of your house! And get your kids away from him!" Bree wanted it to happen now, but Kelsey knew this was going to take some strategic planning.

"I don't think the kids and I are in any danger. Brady loves us…and it's quite obvious he is doing anything to hold on to us and our lives together," Kelsey explained, "Taylor was a threat to our happiness. She was going to uncover his secret. He killed Marty so he could have his wife." Kelsey was reeling. In her mind, this all made sense. Crazy sense. In her heart, however, she was looking for a way out. A way to escape the possibility her husband is a murderer. Kelsey felt sick to her stomach at the thought of it.

Unraveled

"How is this happening? What is he doing to these people while they are under anesthetic?" Now Bree was the one shaking as Kelsey walked over to sit next to her on the couch. She sat close to her and continued talking. "Bailey, my doctor in training, has been helping me to piece this all together. Since Charlie is involved, she is too. Bailey figured out that Brady is using anesthetic to overdose the patients. Thiopental to be exact. Sound familiar?"

"Oh dear God," Bree said, "the same drug he used to induce Kyle's never-ending coma!"

"He is very smart and very good." I need proof, and so far I have the help of his colleague who privately had an autopsy performed on Taylor's body before her funeral. It was definitely a thiopental overdose that killed her," Kelsey told Bree, still feeling that overwhelming sickness in the pit of her stomach.

"Wow, okay, so you have that information?" Bree was surprised at how much has been going on in just a few days since she and Kelsey got away for one night. "Do you have travel proof? Proof that he was in D.C.?"

"I saw the plane ticket stub but I didn't take it. I just looked in his briefcase and it was there. I'm sure he has destroyed it by now. As far as proof that he was at the hospital, both Dr. Reiss and the anesthesiologist saw him and were with him in the operating room. I just can't believe this is happening and I'm scared there is even more I do not know." Kelsey's hands were shaking and Bree took them in hers and held them.

"Me too, and that is why you have to get the police involved," Bree insisted.

"Not yet, and promise me, you won't either. And if you see him, be normal. Please!" Kelsey begged her.

"Well, I am going to see him," Bree said, "because we are all going to be together this weekend for my wedding."

"What?" Kelsey was both surprised and happy.

"Jack and I decided. Fuck it. Why wait any longer? Let's get married. Our life is so crazy together, but it's ours and we want to make it official and become a real family with Sam."

Kelsey was laughing, "Oh that is the best damn news I've heard in days! We will be there. All four of us."

***

And they were. All four of them had happy, proud, smiling faces when Bree and Jack exchanged their vows in an intimate ceremony at a small church in Greenville, New York. Kelsey stood next to Bree, supporting her and loving her, as she pledged her love and committed her life to Jack Logan. He will make a wonderful husband to Bree, Kelsey was thinking as she looked out into the congregation of the small church and saw Brady looking over at her. One year ago, she had believed he too would make a wonderful husband. And he has. That was the most difficult part of all, of everything, that recently came to light. He was good to her and to her kids. He loves them. And they all love him.

Miles was sitting next to Brady and Charlie. Bailey had the job of walking Sam around the church, up and down the side aisles in his umbrella stroller. Bree knew he would be fussy in that environment so she had asked Bailey to keep him moving. And he was doing great.

After the ceremony, they all ended up back at Mr. and Mrs. Logan's home for a catered meal. Before they ate, Kelsey was upstairs with Bree in her bedroom while she was changing into something more casual rather than her short off-white silk dress that she had just gotten married in a few hours earlier. "So, tell me, what has happened in the last few days? Anything new?" Bree was talking quietly as Kelsey walked over to her in the middle of the bedroom.

"I do need to talk to you about something, but not here and not now. Everything, on the surface, is fine, Brady has been normal while Bailey and I continue to pretend all is well." Kelsey rejoined the party with Bree. This was her best friend's special day. She wasn't going to do anything to take the spotlight away from Bree and Jack. She didn't want to tell Bree what was happening. She hadn't told anyone. Yet.

***

It was still so fresh in her mind. He had come to her when she was standing inside of the church and the music began to play. As she walked the length of the aisle, she could see Jack standing there, smiling, with his younger brother at his side. She could see the small crowd in the church turning to look at her. And then she could see him. Clear as day. Kyle.

He was dressed in his tuxedo, just as he had been the day she married him. He, with that sandy blond hair of his, was standing up ahead of her, at the end of the aisle, as if he was waiting for her. Just like on their wedding day. The image of him had faded by the time she reached Jack and his brother. They were waiting for Bree and when the organist began to play the wedding march, Kelsey thought of that day. Their wedding day. This had happened a few times in the last week. Ever since Miles said he had seen his daddy. And ever since Kyle had spoken to him. What Miles had not known was that message was for her, too. Kyle wanted her to know she could get through this. She wanted to talk to him. She wanted him to talk to her, more. He was making *appearances* to her, inside of the church had been the third one, just to remind her he was there. *Or was there something more? Was he trying to tell her something?* She had a strong feeling he was trying to send her a message. Now, she just had to figure out what it could be.

Chapter 17

Following Bree's impromptu wedding, everyone was back to work and in school. Bree and Jack had opted not to take a honeymoon – until Sam is a little bit older and easier to handle. They didn't want to leave him and disrupt his routine. Because, anyone who knows Sam, knows his routine is golden.

Kelsey was wrapping up a meeting in her newspaper office with the mayor of New York City when her cell phone buzzed. When the mayor left soon after, she retrieved her phone. It was a text from Bailey. It was her internship day with Brady, the first with him since she had found out he has been lying to her mother and to her. He wasn't the man she wanted to grow to love as her father. She had been trying, really hard, to overcome that obstacle. In the past few weeks, she had contemplated calling him *dad*. She wanted to feel more like his daughter. Not anymore. And it was getting more difficult for her to keep up this facade with him – all of the time. So she sent her mother a text. *Mom, I need you. I don't know how much longer I can do this. Working with Brady is killing me. I want to be here, but I don't want to be with him. He is in surgery right now. Please meet me for lunch. We can just eat in the hospital cafeteria if you don't have much time.* Kelsey looked at the time on her cell phone. It was eleven forty-five. She texted back, *I will be there at noon*, and she grabbed her Coach purse and walked out of her office.

***

When Kelsey entered the hospital, she wondered how long Brady would be in surgery. She assumed Bailey had invited her to meet for lunch, knowing he would be tied up for awhile. Well, he wasn't. The surgery was complete and he was inside of the office, just three doors ahead on the right, from where Kelsey was walking. It was Mary Sue's office. She had her own office, where Brady often visited when he needed some motherly advice. She most certainly loved that boy – that man – as she does her own three sons. Her boys had all graduated from college, earned their degrees, and moved away from New York City to pursue their careers. And her husband, a truck driver, rarely ever came home. Mary Sue was lonely so she wrapped herself up in her work, and often times in Brady's world. She had missed him when he moved on to Washington University Hospital, but now he is back, and all hers again.

Mary Sue wasn't a cougar after a much younger man, but she would do anything for Brady. To protect him. And that fierce loyalty was born the night in the hospital when she had watched Brady inject thiopental into Kyle Newman's IV. She had unintentionally walked in on Brady, recognized that he appeared to be *caught in the act,* and she confronted him. She had been well aware of the medications being injected into the comatose patient and she didn't hesitate to ask Brady about what she witnessed him doing. He had tried to talk his way out of the situation, but she didn't buy into it. She knew he was lying, and when she told him so, he told her he never had a mother growing up. But, she had become so much like a mother to him, and he needed her to keep his secret. He needed her support because he didn't want to lose the woman he had just fallen so deeply in love with. Mary Sue fell for Brady's words. She was beyond flattered. Her own three sons were distant and unloving, just like their father. She had a desperate need to fill that void in her life. And Brady needed her. Soon after he had gained her trust, Brady knew for certain he could confide in Mary Sue about the file he deleted. He had told her, through his tears, how he wanted Kelsey back in his life and he had just done the unimaginable to try to make that happen. That was a crucial moment in Brady's life. He was feeling remorseful and truly considering telling Kyle Newman what he originally found on the Cat Scan. A part of him wanted to save Kyle's life. His patient's life. He had never before put a patient in harm's way – until Kyle Newman. But a bigger part of him wanted a life with Kelsey. And after Mary Sue listened to Brady, she was the one who convinced him to continue as he knew nothing.

Because he deserved to be with his destiny.

Mary Sue believed in destiny, but she had lost the one chance to find hers. Growing up, she had an older sister who had a steady boyfriend. Mary Sue was a freshman in high school during her older sister's senior year at the same school. Her sister, Betty had been completely infatuated with her boyfriend, Jimmy. And so was Mary Sue. On prom night, Betty was drunk and passed out early, after the dance. Their parents weren't home, so Jimmy stayed to hang out with Mary Sue. He wanted to watch a movie or something on TV. He had been disappointed in Betty. She had promised to give herself to him, but she had too much to drink and their first time didn't happen that night. Mary Sue wanted *her* first time to be special. And so she came on to Jimmy on the couch in their family's living room. Jimmy, at first, balked but Mary Sue persisted, enticed, and eventually was successful at seducing her sister's boyfriend. Betty never found out, and Jimmy never wanted to look back. It only happened once. He called it a mistake, he called Mary Sue a *heartless bitch* for doing that to her own sister. The sister who Jimmy was in love with and eventually married. Mary Sue believed Jimmy was her destiny. She loved him so much more than her sister did. Mary Sue never had a boyfriend or another lover all throughout her high school years, not after that one night with Jimmy. He was, in her mind, the one who got away. When she was in her second year of nursing school, a truck driver had paid attention to her late one night at a diner. His name was Jimmy. And he, forty-one years later, is still Mary Sue's husband. But, he never came close to being the Jimmy she wanted and desired on her sister's prom night. Mary Sue didn't want Brady to live like she had, terribly unhappy for most of her life, so she supported his quest to do *anything* to make Kelsey his again.

Kelsey continued walking until she suddenly caught a glimpse of him through the narrow glass window on Mary Sue's office door. He was sitting on the edge of her desk and she was seated in her chair. He was wearing his tight fitted blue scrubs and he still had on his surgery cap, to match. She passed the door, but stopped. This is a main hallway. It would be obvious to anyone who passed by if she were to just stand there and eavesdrop. The hallway remained empty and she tried to hear them. And that is when she took a chance. She stepped off to the side of the door, so she could not be seen through the window, and then she grabbed the door handle tightly, slowly and carefully turning it while saying a quick prayer that she was not heard. She slightly cracked the door open as the voices coming from inside stopped. If this was it, if they knew she was there, Kelsey had prepared herself for what she would do next. She would just say, *hey, sorry to interrupt, I just popped in for lunch with Bailey, care to join us?* Sure Bailey's plans would be botched, but that white lie would save Kelsey. She, however, did not have to resort to that plan. She heard Mary Sue's voice, so she remained standing near the door. To listen.

"How many times do I have to tell you I'm sorry for telling Kelsey you had not worked all weekend as she and the kids had thought? If you had told me you were taking off to D.C., I could have covered for you again. Don't get all pissy with me. It's your mess again." *For the love of God. Perfect timing.*

Now, please God, keep this hallway empty. At least long enough for me to figure out how to expose my husband for the liar he is.

"Calm down, it's over. I didn't have a chance to tell you when I got back," Brady raised his voice. "I went straight home from the airport. Kelsey never said anything to me about your phone call. And I don't know why. I don't want her to feel like she cannot trust me. She's been fine, like herself, lately so I guess I will just let this go." Listening to his voice, speaking about lying and keeping secrets from her was startling and sad at the same time, for Kelsey. There was no way she could have ever prepared herself for the truths she has uncovered, one after another, in the past few days. And it was about to get worse. Much worse.

"You just better hope that crazy sensitive Elliot can get past what happened in his operating room," Mary Sue continued, "I still cannot believe he didn't see you inject that IV." *Oh my God…to actually hear those words…to know the truth now.* Kelsey put her hand over her mouth as the tears sprung to her eyes. She quickly looked around. No one was coming. And then she listened again. "I think you better give the fucking thiopental a rest now, son. First, all of those years ago with Kyle Newman, then with Marty Sutter, and now with Taylor Barton. Stop while you're ahead, for chrissake."

"I didn't overdose Kyle Newman. I just used it to keep him under long enough," Brady stated, sounding annoyed.

"You got the girl, baby boy," Mary Sue said to him and Kelsey wanted to throw up. She also wanted to peek inside that window. Was he sitting on her fucking lap like a good little boy? She sure was crawling up his ass – and must have been for many years. She knew *his* story. She knew *his* past. And apparently it is a very dark past.

"Yes, I did, but I had to wait *too long* for her. He raised my daughter. He had my wife in his arms, in his bed every goddamn night. Too bad some people can live with aneurysms longer than others." Kelsey felt her knees give out. Her feet were no longer steady on the floor. She fell back, up against the wall, trying to remain standing as her body was buckling.

But, she was still listening.

"You're just damn lucky no one knew you read that scan and saw an aneurysm tucked inside Kyle Newman's brain, causing him chronic headaches," Mary Sue said, sounding like she wanted to scold Brady but she had laughter in her voice. It was sickening to hear, and it was taking everything Kelsey had inside of her at that moment just to keep herself upright. Brady had known all along why Kyle was suffering from those headaches. He had known, year after year, that Kyle's days were numbered. If only they had gotten a second opinion. If only Kyle would have complained more and told her he was in pain. She truly believed he was not in constant pain. He had told her, more than once, through their married years, that it was a pain he could handle. Sometimes it was gone for awhile, and other times it was just a dull ache. He reassured her, time and again, it was nothing a little ibuprofen couldn't take care of. Kyle could have been taken care of though. He could still be alive, if it hadn't been for Brady. Brady's lie. Brady's cover up. Brady's deceit.

"Mrs. Walker, are you okay?" Kelsey's thoughts were interrupted and the eavesdropping was over. A nurse, who she remembered as Carrie, was standing before her with concern.

"Oh my gosh, yes, I need to eat something, that's all. I'm on my way into the cafeteria to meet my daughter for some lunch. I shouldn't do that to myself. Thanks, Carrie…" Kelsey finished her words as she walked off. She had to get away from that door. She had to pull herself together and get to Bailey.

And Bailey knew something was very wrong the moment she saw her. "Mom? Jesus, sit down, you look awful." Kelsey sat down and Bailey sat close to her. "What is going on?"

"I'm here to support you and get you through your day," Kelsey said, trying very hard to hold it together in front of her daughter. She had to. Brady was just down the hall. This was not the time or place to unravel.

"Okay, well, let's just get each other through this. How much longer before we involve the police? Mom, this hurts like hell, but we have to get him out of our lives." This was one of those times, and there have been many moments like this for Kelsey, where she didn't feel like the mother in their relationship. She was learning from her daughter. Her daughter was the brave, smart, girl who knew how to move on. And survive.

"I need to get Elliot's proof, from the autopsy," Kelsey explained, "I told him I would call him when I am ready."

"Ready for what?" Neither Kelsey nor Bailey had seen him walk up to their table, but they were both startled by Brady's voice – and he noticed. "My goodness, what has you two so jumpy today?"

"We just didn't see you coming," Kelsey said, as he sat down in the other chair beside her and Bailey agreed, "Yeah, Brady, I called mom for lunch because I thought you would be in surgery longer and we were just catching up and talking about how we think Miles is ready for a traveling basketball team, you know, in addition to his school team." Kelsey was amazed at how her daughter could think on her feet. She had hoped she inherited that trait from her – being a clever, quick-thinking investigative reporter at times – and not from her father. Because, apparently, *he* was a real talent at saying and doing anything to get people to believe him. And to believe in him.

Brady continued to talk about how he most definitely thought Miles could handle being on another team, and Bailey kept that conversation going. None of them had any food in front of them yet and Kelsey was going to suggest they eat something because she was still feeling so light-headed from the shock earlier. But that's when Brady's cell phone buzzed. He took the call right there at the table as Kelsey and Bailey glanced at each other with wide eyes. And then Brady ended the call quickly and put Bailey to work. "Lunch is going to have to wait a little bit kiddo, I need you to see Nurse Carrie for me. She has a patient scheduled for me to see in fifteen minutes. He's having an allergic reaction to his antibiotic. Your job is to see him with Nurse Carrie and I want you to relay everything, all of his side effects, to me when I get in there." That was Nurse Carrie's job, but Brady has been making Bailey do more hands-on work lately and she was enjoying it. She said she would do it, and left the table after giving her mom a tight hug, and telling her she would *talk to her later.*

"Shouldn't she be able to eat lunch first?" Kelsey asked Brady, feeling unnerved at how her daughter was chased away.

"She can in less than a half hour. Carrie just called me because I had asked her to. I wanted to know when my patient arrived so I could send Bailey in to take the reins. I already know the man is allergic to penicillin and will need an antibiotic lacking that."

Kelsey smiled, and he came toward her, to kiss her. She briefly met his lips with hers, but then pulled away. "Brady, not here," she said to him, wiping her lips off with her fingers.

"Then, later, at home. It's been too long, babe. You've either been on your period this past week or complaining of a sore throat, afraid you're going to get me sick. I'm going to get blue balls if you make me wait any longer." Kelsey laughed at him. *You're going to get more than blue balls, you son of a bitch.*

Chapter 18

She hadn't told Bailey about Brady's lie of omission that inevitably murdered Kyle. She did tell Bree. She needed to tell someone, and Bree has always been her go-to person. Especially when her life is unraveling. Bree completely flipped out. The two of them were standing in their cul-de-sac, in the middle of the street in between their houses, when Bree told her to end this now. *Get the proof and get that bastard out of your life. Out of all of our lives. He deserves to rot in jail for the rest of his life!*

Handling this alone was probably not the best idea she ever had, Kelsey knew, but she also knew Brady and how well he could talk his way out of any situation. A life is a life and no matter if it was Marty's or Taylor's, or both, Kelsey knew Brady had to pay for what he did to them and to their families. But, now, it sent her reeling knowing it was Kyle's life he also had a hand in ending. She finished talking to Bree, again making her swear not to tell a soul – not even Jack. Especially Jack, because he would try to rip Brady apart. Everyone was going to be hurt when the truth came out, but no one more than Kelsey. She went upstairs into her old bedroom, the bedroom she had shared with Kyle, and she closed the door. It was Bailey's room now and she had gone in there for a reason. She picked up another framed picture off of her daughter's dresser. It was of herself and Kyle, and she held it close to her chest as she made her way over to the bed, and finally lost it. Everything she had learned in the last week had finally boiled over. She was sobbing uncontrollably and scared to death of what was about to happen to her life. Again, she would be alone with her children, with a broken heart. She cried until she felt as if she didn't have any tears left. And that's when he walked in the room.

When he saw her, he immediately ran to her and sat beside her on the bed. "What is the matter? Please tell me…it kills me to see your face wet with tears like this. Come on, babe, I love you…we can get through anything." Brady attempted to hold her, but she abruptly pulled away from him and stood up.

"Don't. Don't touch me. Ever again." She couldn't do it anymore. This started nearly twenty years ago, between them, and it was going to end the same way, *just between them.* The police would have to get involved later. Kelsey had her proof now, and she wanted to deal with him. Alone.

Brady was confused, "Ever again? I don't know what is going on here, but I deserve an explanation." Kelsey was up, on her feet, and Brady was still sitting on the end of the bed, staring at her with confusion all over his face.

"Oh, so, this is about what *you* deserve? I think it's the other way around, Brady Walker. I deserved so much better than this. Once again, I'm left reeling because of your dishonesty…and so much more. I am such a fool for believing in you and loving you." Brady was scared. He had rushed home as soon as Nurse Carrie told him she had seen his wife in the hallway, outside of Mary Sue's office door. She had told him it was obvious his wife was either ill or reacting to something terrible. She then told him it was apparent his wife was eavesdropping on his conversation with Mary Sue. Brady had panicked. He knew what they were talking about. They very rarely ever discussed his past, but Mary Sue's most recent slip up on the phone with Kelsey had made Brady angry and nervous. He wanted to make sure she understood to never let anything like that happen again. Kelsey was his world and he was not going to lose her. All the while he was driving home, he was trying his damndest not to freak out. *What if she knew the truth? And how is he going to save his marriage if she does?*

"Take a little trip back in time with me…in your mind, flip to the day that Kyle had his CAT Scan at Laneview

Hospital. What did you tell him?" Kelsey's eyes were wild with anger and she never took them off of her husband. Brady remained calm, but he feared everything he treasured in his life was about to go up in flames.

He stood up to stand before her. He always looked her in the eye. He always could look directly at her, and lie. "I did see the results of that scan on that day, and as you know, I told Kyle he was clear. I did not know what was causing his chronic headaches. But, you have to understand, doctors do not always see what is there. I mean, sometimes an aneurysm can hide itself. I'm sure you will always wonder if it was there all along, but that is something we will never know."

"No, we know!" Kelsey snapped at him, "I just found out, but *you* have always known. Isn't that right, Brady? Maybe I should give mama bear Mary Sue a call and see if she would like to add anything to this conversation? Oh, no, wait, I think she said quite enough today in her office with you!" This was it. This was going to be damn near impossible for Brady to talk his way out of.

"So you overheard us talking? It's not what you're thinking, please just let me explain." At that moment, he had nothing to explain. There were no words in his mind or rolling off of his tongue. He was caught and he was feeling lost, and Kelsey was so consumed with anger she couldn't see the true panic on his face.

"It's not what I'm thinking? Do you even know what I'm *thinking* right now, Brady? I'm thinking I need to get you the hell away from me and from my children! I'm thinking you said you loved us, all of us, and you betrayed us! You are a fucking liar, a con man, a son of a bitch who also happens to be a murderer!" She was screaming at him, and what she did not know is Bailey and Charlie were one floor below them. It was taking everything Charlie had to keep Bailey from racing up the stairs. She wanted to save her mother, but Charlie physically had his arms around her, repeatedly reminding Bailey this is her mother's battle. She needed to handle her husband, alone. They would stay there, and be there, in the house, if she needed help. And they continued to listen to them. And all the while Charlie was encouraging Bailey, telling her everything is going to be alright, he felt just as scared as she did. The family he had grown to love and feel so much a part of was unraveling.

"A murderer?" was all he had asked. He now knew she was speaking of more than just Kyle Newman. His wife, a seasoned reporter, had obviously done some investigating. He wondered, and he feared, just how much she had uncovered.

"Yes! A murderer! Shall I name your victims, Dr. Walker? Marty Sutter! Taylor Barton! And *my* husband! The man I was grieving for when you walked back into my life, and I believed you helped me to heal from the pain of losing him. I believed it all, I believed...you..." her voice trailed off and suddenly she could not keep from crying. She was in so much pain. And so was he.

He walked over to her and stood close. His voice was calm and quiet. "My greatest fear is losing you. And the life we have built together with the kids. You know I love both of them, Miles is an amazing little boy, and Bailey is mine. You told me the truth about her so we could spend the rest of our lives together, as a family. Do not take that away from me. Do not walk away from me again, because I swear to you, on my mother's grave, I cannot handle that. I will not live without you and our kids." Tears were welling up in his eyes. Those bright crystal blue eyes.

Kelsey was crying hard and he wanted to take her into his arms and fall completely apart with her, and then find a way to pick up all of the pieces to put back together their love story. Their life together. "Help me to be a better man. Help me be the man you deserve. I can't explain it, I feel like something overtakes my mind and my body when I feel the threat of losing you. I need you, in order to survive. Please help me…" He was choking on his tears and Kelsey was feeling just as lost as he sounded. She couldn't fall into that trap again. She loved him. So much. But he was not the man she believed him to be. Yes, he needed help. But, there wasn't anything more she could do for him. For them. For their marriage. And for their family. She wanted out. And she wanted him out of all of their lives.

She was extremely relieved at this moment she had told Bree about the email Elliot Reiss sent to her after she left the hospital today, after she had called him to tell him she was ready to get justice. For Marty. For Taylor. And, especially, for Kyle. Bree now had a copy of that email, which contained the autopsy proof of Taylor Barton's thiopental overdose, just in case something were to happen to Kelsey. Bree, however, was not going to allow anything to happen to her. Bree knew exactly how Kelsey reacted to Brady Walker. She knew the hold he once had on her, and now that hold appeared to be even stronger.

Brady pulled her close, into his arms, and she allowed him to. She was feeling incredibly weak, and crying with him. She had her eyes closed, as they both tightened their arms around each other. And when she opened her eyes, she saw the picture on the bed that she had been clenching earlier. Kyle was looking right at her, from that photograph, and if he could have spoken to her at that moment, she knew what he would have said. *Don't do this. Save yourself. Save our kids. Get him the hell out of your life.*

Strength from Kyle enabled Kelsey to do what she did next. She pulled away from her husband quickly and then very calmly told him, "Get out of my life, get out of my house. It is only a matter of time before you lose everything. Your job. And your freedom." Brady knew then Kelsey was planning to involve the police. He had just hoped he had some time. He had hoped she hadn't turned him in yet.

"No!" he reacted with a panic in his voice Kelsey had never heard from him before. "I will not let you keep me from my daughter! She is mine, goddammit she is mine! I am so fucking fed up with losing in this life, no matter what I do, I always end up losing! I will not let you do this to me!" Brady lunged toward her with a force that almost threw Kelsey backwards, but he had ahold of her by the shoulders and he wasn't letting her go.

With that, the door flew open and Brady turned around to see Bailey standing there, and Charlie was not too far behind her. "Let go of my mother and do as she said, get out of our house, and out of our lives." There was a strength in that young girl, at this very moment, Kelsey had never seen before.

"Bailey, honey, we can all work this out," Brady released his hands from gripping Kelsey's shoulders, and he walked toward his daughter. "Come on, please, we just found each other, I'm your dad." Kelsey was watching them, and so was Charlie. He had his cell phone in his hand, ready to call the police. He knew, eventually, they all were going to need protection from this man. He just couldn't believe what was happening to this family. None of them could.

"No. My dad held me the moment I was born. My dad sat in the rocking chair in my nursery in the middle of the night, comforting me when I had my first fever from cutting teeth. My dad taught me how to color inside of the lines, how to ride a bike, how to hit a ball, and how to be kind to others. My dad taught me right from wrong. *You* are not my dad, and *you* never will be. I hate how I fell for your facade. I hate how I wanted to be just like you, a good doctor. And I hate you." Bailey never once raised her voice or moved from where she was standing. But, Brady looked like a man who had been torn apart. Beaten to a pulp. His daughter's words broke him. He turned to Kelsey, one last time, with tears streaming down his face, and he said, "I am so very sorry."

As he walked away, he passed his daughter without uttering another word, and he didn't look at her. He couldn't. He had failed her. He had failed his own flesh and blood. He walked down the stairs of the home he would never again live in, he left behind his wife and his daughter, who were both holding each other and crying, uncontrollably. Bailey had fallen completely apart when Brady walked out of the room and she ran to her mother's open arms. This was killing both of them.

When Brady reached the front door, he opened it, and found himself face to face with a man. He had a shaved head and a muscular body. Brady met his height and was equally as toned, but this man had anger in his eyes and Brady had absolutely no idea who he was standing there with. Kyle had loved this guy for years. Nicholas Bridges was his best friend and partner in solving crime and seeing justice served.

When Kelsey heard his voice, she grabbed Bailey by the hand and Charlie followed them swiftly down the stairs. "Brady Walker, you are under arrest for the murder of Taylor Barton – and two more people we may never be able to prove you son of a bitch, but if it's the last fucking thing I do, I will see to it that you rot in prison for the rest of your life for what you did to Kyle Newman." Kelsey watched Nicholas handcuff Brady right there in her living room. She could not believe *he* was there.

He was there because Bree was not going to stand by and do nothing. She knew, all too well, how Kelsey reacted to Brady Walker. She knew, deep down, Kelsey could never turn him in to the authorities. She had watched her spend days putting off a confrontation with Brady. And maybe she was right to do that. Maybe it happened for a reason. Because today she had discovered the complete truth when she learned how Brady had always known Kyle would eventually die of a brain aneurysm. So Bree did the only thing she knew she could do. She hadn't seen him since the day after they buried their son. And she had intended to spend the rest of her life without ever having to see him again. Until today. Until she dialed the number of the New York City Police Department, said it was urgent, and asked for Detective Nicholas Bridges. He was floored to hear her voice on the other end of the phone. She had gotten right to the point. *Kelsey is in trouble. Her husband is a murderer and your best friend is dead because of him.*

Bree explained the rest of the story after Nicholas came directly to her house. He had heard she was living right across the street from Kelsey. He also heard she had a new man in her life, and a baby boy. It pained him to know he is the reason Bree had lost *their* boy. Max was thirteen years old when he died as a result of a car accident. Nicholas had given his irresponsible older daughter, a former drug addict and unreachable soul, permission to drive their son to school. That ride had cost Max his life. And that decision had cost Nicholas his marriage, and his family.

"Nicholas! Wait, do you have what you need?" Kelsey meant the proof, which she had emailed to Bree and had no idea Bree would use it to contact the police. Especially Nicholas.

"I have it, yes." Nicholas looked directly at Kelsey, and for the first time ever he saw something in her eyes. He didn't know if he was seeing gratitude, relief, or maybe she had finally liked him. Maybe they had finally met each other halfway. In the name of justice. For the sake of Kyle.

And then he walked away, with Brady willingly at his side. As he was placing Brady in the back seat of his unmarked police car, Bree was running up the driveway and into Kelsey's arms. "Thank God, you're safe. I had no other choice, I had to do something. You better know damn well I would do anything for you now. I called my loser ex for help." The two of them managed to smile a little at each other and Bree wrapped her arms around Kelsey just as she was looking over at Brady, watching her through the window of the backseat. Kelsey looked away quickly. She couldn't do that to herself. She wouldn't remember him, and them, like this. She wanted to thank Bree for doing *this* for her. She wanted to tell her there was no way she could have done it. She wanted to, but that man had a hold on her like she had never known before. She wanted him out of her life now, yes, and she had clearly translated that message to him, but calling the authorities, putting him in prison, was not something she felt she was strong enough to undertake. And Bree knew that. That is why she did it for her. Standing there as Nicholas drove away with Brady in police custody, Bree pulled Kelsey closer and whispered, "It's going to be okay. You are going to be okay."

***

As Nicholas drove through traffic in New York City, he started to come out of the shock of what just happened. He had not said another word to Brady Walker, who was sitting in the back seat of his unmarked squad car. The front and back seat was not divided with the protective steel mesh cage because Nicholas' job, as the lead detective on the police force, never required him to transport criminals. He did always carry a gun and handcuffs. And those handcuffs had come in handy today. He was going to make *that bastard* pay.

What he didn't know is when he had chosen to cuff Brady Walker – with his hands in front of him instead of behind his back, because he had been entirely cooperative at the time of his arrest – it had been a bad move. A mistake that was going to cost him.

As Nicholas came upon a red light and braked to stop the car, Brady gained enough leverage and momentum in the cramped backseat to launch an attack on him. Brady wasted no time moving up against the seat, behind him, and he swung his cuffed hands over Nicholas' head and began putting pressure on his throat. Nicholas had managed to shift the car into park before he grabbed Brady's cuffed hands, at the wrists, and tried to release his grip. The death grip he had around his neck. It seemed like endless minutes, but it had only been seconds before Nicholas felt himself losing the fight. He appeared to slip into unconsciousness as Brady loosened his grip and pulled his arms away from Nicholas's neck, and then he opened his car door. He shut the door behind him and immediately opened Nicholas' driver's side door. Cars were honking as the light had just turned green and Brady hurried to undo the seatbelt on Nicholas' body and then he abruptly pulled him out of the car. His body was still lying on the road as Brady looked into the rearview mirror and frantically sped away.

He was not an escaped criminal, he was not going to spend the rest of his life running and hiding. He is a man who just lost his wife, his daughter, his family, everything he had. He knew next he would lose his job. His successful medical career was over.

He didn't drive far before he threw the car into park and walked a ways uphill to her grave. He stood there for a moment, without moving, without talking. Bailey Melanie Walker. She was only thirty-three years old when she died. When she left him. It pained Brady to visit her gravesite so he had stopped. It had been years, probably since he was a teenager, since he had been back there.

And, finally, he spoke to her.

"I'll bet you saw this coming, all along. I've lost everything because of what you did to me. You have to know by now that you, leaving me when I was only six years old, ruined me. I never again could handle loss. I felt like I had a right to hold onto anything I wanted, and I did absolutely anything to claim and keep what I wanted, what was mine. At any cost. Lives were lost because of me. And I didn't care. Because I got what I wanted, I was protecting what was mine." Tears were streaming down Brady's face. "Yes, mom, it's because of you that I have never been good at letting go. It's because of you that I've left scratches on anything I've been forced to let slip through my hands. I held on so fucking tight, clawing and fighting to hang on, because I couldn't bear to feel that kind of loss again. I just lost my wife, the one woman who completed me. She gave me a daughter, I had a real family, but my web of lies and my covered-up crimes caught up with me. My life is over."

As he said those words, he was choking back his sobs, and he reached on top of his mother's headstone and picked up the handgun he had laid there when he first walked up. His hands were shaking. It was Nicholas Bridges' gun and he had taken it from him after he pulled him out of the car and let his body fall onto the street. He had never in his life held a gun. His weapon of choice was a syringe, an easier way to go, a cleaner way, but he didn't have any other means right now. And he was running out of time. He is a wanted man. At least somebody had still *wanted* him now, he thought, as he pictured Kelsey one last time before he pointed the gun at himself and fired it.

Chapter 19

Kelsey rushed through the emergency doors of Laneview Hospital, with Bree at her side. He had not been admitted yet, just examined by a doctor in the emergency room just moments earlier. When the two women walked into that exam room, they found him sitting up on the table, shirt off. Kelsey had not noticed him having a tattoo before, and Bree was thinking she knew he hadn't. It was on his chest, over his heart, and it was a cross with the name *Maxwell* encircling it. Nicholas Bridges had gotten a permanent marking on his body, in honor of the son he lost too soon.

"So what kind of a loser police detective lets the criminal get away?" Bree was half kidding and half serious. She could not believe Brady had gotten away, but she was relieved to see Nicholas alive. Had he died, from strangulation in that car, she would have felt at fault because she is the one who involved him in Brady's demise.

"It's nice to know you care, Bree," Nicholas smirked and Kelsey spoke next.

"So where is he?" Did she really want to know? She assumed he was on the run. She assumed she could expect him to contact her in the days, weeks, or months ahead. He would want her help. And a part of her would be too damn tempted to help him. She wanted him out of her life, but it was going to take a long time to get him off of her mind and out of her heart. Maybe she would *never* get over him. She hated him for what he did, but she also knew she would always love him as the man she thought he was.

"I faked unconsciousness so he would not kill me," Nicholas started to explain, "and when he took off with my car, I used my cell to call for back up. We found my car not too far away, at the public cemetery." Kelsey looked puzzled and then it quickly hit her. Brady said he would never go back there, it was just too hard, but he must have gone anyway.

"So he's in custody again?" Bree interrupted, "Thank God!" Nicholas looked at them both and he had an expression on his face even Bree had not recognized. She suddenly felt panicked as she glanced over at Kelsey. "Brady took my gun when he left me on the street," Nicholas could hardly say it. It had been an awful sight. Not that he had not seen enough crime scenes of all varieties, but this one was just sad. Lying dead on the ground near his mother's grave, this man, a doctor, wearing blood-stained scrubs from his own violent bloodshed. "He shot himself at his mother's grave. I'm sorry, Kelsey, he's dead." Nicholas had tears in his eyes as he spoke those words and watched Bree bolt toward her dear friend who was, again, on the hospital floor, consumed with shock, anger, and grief.

It took awhile before Kelsey could stop sobbing. Bree had just sat on the floor with her, and held her, rocking her back and forth, giving in to her own tears as well. Nicholas didn't move from the exam table, and he wished he could have walked away. Out of that room. These two women had seen enough grief in their lives and now they were facing it again. He was amazed at their strength and how when one was weak, the other was strong. That is how it worked for true friends. And thinking of that made Nicholas ache for his best friend. Kyle had been gone for almost three years and he missed him as much as he missed his son. His life is so different now. He's alone, and always drinking too much. His job is all he has. Savannah, his twenty-year-old daughter, moved away with a boyfriend she barely knew, and he had not seen or heard from her in almost a year. Nicholas didn't have much purpose left in his life, but when Bree called him for his help today – he felt himself come alive again. He wanted to help. He wanted to see justice for Kyle, and he wanted to protect Kelsey. Now, however, he wondered what would happen to her, consumed with grief for another husband. This time, he had hoped, it would be different for her – considering she now knew the truth. That man was no good for her. Or for himself. Which is why he had taken his own life. Nicholas understood and knew that feeling all too well.

"What am I going to tell my kids?" Kelsey asked Bree when she finally caught her breath. She felt light-headed and spent and she just wanted to lie down and sleep, and maybe wake up to find this had all been a nightmare. *A nightmare. You can say that again.*

"The truth," Bree answered, "Help them understand, this was not just a father figure in their lives who was taken away from them because it was *his time*. This was a man who, come to find out, was a tortured soul and he took his own life to find peace – and to give all of us the same."

"I know you're right," Kelsey said wishing she had better understood Brady's pain and torment – while he was alive. She had absolutely no idea. It was as if he were two different people. "I know losing his medical license would have killed him, I know the humiliation alone would not have been something he could have handled. He needed me, and wanted Miles and especially Bailey in his life more than anything in the world. I do understand why he did it. What I don't understand is how I am expected to get through this kind of pain again. I don't have it in me anymore. I swear to God, I don't…" her words trailed off and Bree was quick to snap her out of that mindset.

"The hell you don't! You listen to me, dammit, you are strong and you have two healthy, good-hearted children who will be depending on you to get it together during this crisis and keep it together. I know this isn't the same damn thing, not by a long shot, but having Sam and dealing with not knowing what lies ahead for him, or for me taking care of him, makes me spiral out of control sometimes but I know I have to put one foot in front of the other, one day at a time. And you have to do the same."

Kelsey stood up with Bree as the ER nurse came into the room to tell Nicholas he is free to go home. He was given a prescription cream to treat the marks, which resembled rug burns, on his neck, from Brady's handcuffs.

"Nicholas," Kelsey said, "is he here? Is Brady's...body...here?" Nicholas shook his head yes, and Bree blurted out, "No! You are not doing that. Leave it alone, Kel. Walk away with me. Now."

"I can't. Wait for me." And that is all Kelsey said before she walked out the door and down the hallway. She took the elevator down to the basement. To the morgue. And when the elevator door opened, she saw her. Mary Sue. She looked disheveled and forlorn, and Kelsey instantly felt sick to her stomach. What kind of a woman supported the crimes of a man, young enough to be her own son? If she had cared, truly cared, about Brady at all, she never would have let any of it go on.

"Kelsey, I'm so sorry for your loss," Mary Sue could

barely get the words out, crying, and dabbing her eyes and her nose with a wadded up, already damp, tissue. "I loved him like he was my–"

"Shut up!" Kelsey snapped at her. No one else was around, but she didn't care if anyone had heard her. "I know the truth, I know you knew everything he did and you stood by, patted him on the head like a good boy, and watched him unravel. He needed help and you fucking let him continue to corrupt himself. You disgust me!" Kelsey pushed past that woman, knocking shoulders with her, as she continued to cry harder. Mary Sue knew exactly what she had done, and she was heartbroken to have just come from seeing *her boy* – like that.

When Kelsey opened the door, she again had feelings of deja vu. *Holy Christ, another young husband gone too soon.* This one, however, had brought death on himself. So was it as sad? Yes, it was, but it was different. Everything had always been different with Brady. The conversations, the instant attraction with a fire that never lost its spark, the intense sex, and that constant overwhelming feeling of being wildly addicted to him, body and soul. His body had not yet been tended to. There was no sterile white sheet. And he was not naked. He was still wearing his scrubs, blood-stained. She feared what she would see when she looked at him. She had imagined his head and face unrecognizable from the bullet's damage. But, that wasn't the case. Brady had shot himself in the heart. How ironic, Kelsey had thought, when she saw his blood-stained scrubs covering his chest. A man who had loved her with his whole heart blew his own heart to bits as he left this world, and her, behind. Maybe he had not wanted to take his love for her, with him, when he died. Maybe he wanted to leave it all behind in order to find peace.

Kelsey was relieved to see his face, intact, one last time. It was scruffy again. He had been busy working long hours, through the night, and he hadn't shaved in a few days. She touched his face with her fingers, and then traced his lips. His eyes, those bright crystal blue eyes, were closed. For the last time.

In there, with him, she felt cold, hateful, and heartless. He had made her feel that way about him. She didn't want to feel those emotions, that is not who she is, but maybe it was easier to feel that way. Toward him.

She wasn't crying when she walked away from him, but she did stop to look back at him, one last time, from across the room. And then she spoke to him. It only felt right to say something before she closed that door. "You came into my life like a whirlwind and you're leaving the same way. Know that I will always love you and remember you as the man I wanted you to be, the man you *were* to me. Find peace, babe."

***

While Kelsey was downstairs in the hospital morgue, Bree was still with Nicholas in the exam room. The doctor released him, and he was standing up, about to put on his shirt. And that is when Bree walked over to him and touched him. She placed her finger on the ink on his chest, on the cross, and then she outlined the letters that spelled out their son's name.

Nicholas did not move. He was taken aback though. He never thought he would see her again. And now she was touching him, and somehow he knew right then and right there they were finally going to have a chance to find some closure, together.

"You wanted to keep him close to your heart this way?" Bree asked, taking her hand away from his skin, and feeling chill bumps on her arms.

"Yes, you know I've always wanted a tat and it just seemed like a good way to honor our boy, I remember him every time I look in the mirror. Not that I don't think of him every second of every day anyway, but you know what I mean."

"All too well," Bree agreed, "I hope you're happy-" she started to say and he interrupted her, "With myself? Never. I will never be happy with how it all ended. It was my fault, I am the reason Max died and I am completely to blame for our marriage falling apart. I should have been a better father to him, and a worthy husband to you." Bree could not believe his honest words. Loss changed him. And she was, at this very moment, so grateful for the chance to let go of the hate in her heart that she had been carrying for this man, her ex-husband, ever since they buried their son.

"I think life has thrown too much shit at all of us, and I think it's time you and I agree it was God's plan for Max to live for thirteen years with us – and then God would take him back," Bree said those words with an overwhelming need to make peace with Nicholas, and to help him forgive himself. "No matter who told him it was okay to get in that jeep. No matter who was driving. Max was not going to come back to us, that day. God allocated him thirteen years. It was his time. I believe that now."

Nicholas had tears streaming down his cheeks. The only other time Bree had seen him cry was when their son died. "You've forgiven me. You were so angry, and you had every right to be… but I need you to know I would have switched places with him in an instant to bring our boy back to you." Now Bree was crying too, and when he opened his arms to her, she fell into them.

And that is when Kelsey walked back into the exam room. She just stood there, watching them. She knew they had finally found closure. Forgiveness. Peace. She saw their tears, witnessed their embrace, and walked back out of the door feeling the same way. Like a chapter had finally been closed. And it was time to begin another. Peacefully.

Chapter 20

D r. Brady Walker's funeral was private. There was no funeral home viewing, no ceremony in a church. Just a burial. His body was buried in the cemetery plot right beside his mother's. Kelsey and her children, and Bree and Jack, did go to the cemetery for a blessing led by a minister and they each set a rose on his coffin, before they walked away and he was put into his final resting place.

Kelsey explained to her kids not to dwell on how Brady's life had ended, but to remember the good in him, the love he had shown all of them. Kelsey and Bailey talked at length in the days following Brady's suicide. Bailey still wanted to pursue a medical career. She wanted to become a doctor before she met Brady, and she still did. She would always remember what he taught her during their time spent inside those hospital walls. She finally knew the entire story, how Brady had drugged her father – and then later kept a crucial fact from him after he detected a brain aneurysm on the CAT Scan. It was extremely difficult for her to accept that her biological father had been partly responsible for the death of her dad. It was equally as difficult for her to comprehend how Brady abused his medical license. He was supposed to help and to heal his patients. She believed her mom when she said Brady was a tortured soul. He meant well, but his demons overcame him. Focusing on his good is now the only way to move forward, and Bailey was going to do just that.

It was Miles who Kelsey had been more worried about. He didn't know the whole story and she believed he was too young to be told all of it. But, she was wrong. Her little boy needed to know that it was *not* God's will for Brady to be taken away from them. Brady was the one who made that selfish decision. He could have owned up to his mistakes, his crimes, but he took a coward's way out. Kelsey wanted to explain that to Miles and when she tried to, he had surprised her with his full understanding of it all.

"I will miss him, mom," Miles had said to her, "but not the way I miss my daddy every day." Kelsey looked at him wondering why he felt that way, and Miles explained. "I know he killed himself. I know he did some bad things and ended up feeling like there was no hope."

"Miles, who told you this?" Kelsey knew there were rumors circling, but she had not waited long to sit Miles down and tell him Brady was gone.

"Dad did."

Kelsey froze, "He did?"

"Yes, he came to me, in my bedroom, and he talked to me. He stayed for a long time. He reminded me that I am the man of the house now. He said life doesn't always work out the way we want it to, but I am going to have a good life – and so are you and Bailey." There were no tears from Miles this time. No intensity, like the last time his dad appeared to him. Kyle had given his son exactly what he needed to get through the pain of losing Brady. He gave him the gift of himself by appearing to him and speaking the truth. Miles needed Kyle and he was blessed with exactly that. His dad's angelic presence, his dad's words of wisdom, his dad's promise to always be with him, had saved Miles.

***

So her children were going to be okay. Kelsey was too. It was just a matter of getting there. Getting to the point of believing it. And, she knew, she was going to need some help with that.

Their house was again rearranged to make another change easier for all of them. Miles remained in his same bedroom, and Bailey returned to her old bedroom to allow her mom to have her upstairs master bedroom back. Kelsey had not gone back to her bedroom downstairs, the bedroom she had shared with Brady. She only walked in there once to gather all of her clothes and other belongings and then she walked out and shut the door. She also shut the door to Brady's office. The basement, those two rooms, were going to be off limits to her for awhile. Maybe forever. She needed to get the point of being able to handle all that had happened, all that had unraveled, and again she wanted help with doing that.

That is where Dr. Judy Winthrop fit back into the picture.

Kelsey was, once again, back inside of her office. She had stopped seeing her psychiatrist when Brady returned and found a place in her life again. Dr. Judy was pleased, then, to see Kelsey healing and to know she was moving on, married again. In love again. Happy again.

But, now, she was once again worried about Kelsey's survival plan. Dr. Judy was professionally affected by the death of Dr. Brady Walker. She heard the rumors, most of them true. Kelsey had been lied to, deceived, in the worst possible way. And she was expecting Kelsey's call. Or, she had at least hoped for it. And prayed for her in the meantime.

Kelsey noticed the dark rimmed glasses on Dr. Judy's beautiful face. They were new, and they accented her short, black, spikey hair and bold eyes. "I guess you know why I'm here, back on your couch, looking for some way to erase the pain, and heal," Kelsey seemed more together to Dr. Judy than before. The death, the suicide, of her second husband had not seemed to rock her world. It just appeared, to Dr. Judy, like Kelsey had already found some sort of closure in an effort to accept this tragedy, and move on.

"What kind of pain are you in?" Dr. Judy asked her, "Are you in that same sink hole as you were when you lost Kyle? Are you suppressing your feelings from everyone, from yourself?"

"No, it's not like that this time. Not at all," Kelsey explained, "My feelings are out there. My children know the full extent of everything that happened, and we are all trying to put it behind us."

Dr. Judy was pleased to hear that, but puzzled as to why Kelsey seemed in such a rush. It had only been two weeks since her husband took his own life. "This isn't going to go away overnight," she quietly told her, "You and your children are going to reel from the shock of it for awhile. You're going to still miss him in your lives, in your house, in your hearts. He was, despite his demons, a good person. At least he showed you and your children that he could be."

"I know…and I find myself remembering all of the good, all of the love, but if I dwell, I know I will begin to miss him more than I already do. I think it's easier to hate what he did right now," Kelsey admitted, "It's easier to focus on how much damage he did, rather than allow myself to continue to love and miss the hell out of that man." Kelsey was not crying, but her eyes showed pain. She was incredibly hurt by Brady, and because of that pain she had closed herself off to the possibility of ever allowing another man into her life. And into her heart.

"That is okay, do that right now if you need to," Dr. Judy said to her as she reached for her hand while sitting next to her on the couch in her office. "But, you must also remember, you are worthy of more happiness and more love in your life. You have a lot of living left to do, my dear, and you are not to let Brady keep you from doing it. Give yourself time to heal."

***

Kelsey walked away feeling better. She knew she was worthy, but all she wanted to do now is continue to raise her children, give them a good life, a stable home, love them unconditionally, and always believe what Kyle had told their son. *Life doesn't always work out the way we want it to, but you all are going to have a good life.*

She was walking through the south wing of the hospital when she heard a voice behind her. "Kelsey?" She turned around and she wasn't sure who had just called her name. A man, in a white lab coat, had stopped her. "Yes?" And then he walked closer and she recognized his face. It was his hair that caught her eye though. It was different from the one and only time she had met him.

"Remember me? Elliot Reiss." Elliot held out his hand to her, and she took it. "Of course. My goodness, how are you?" Kelsey assumed a medical conference had brought him to New

York City. Maybe the same type that brought him there a year ago when Brady invited him to their home for dinner. She liked Elliot that evening, she enjoyed his company. He is a brilliant man, a skilled doctor. He practiced general medicine and is a heart specialist. And what she didn't know is he had just been hired as Laneview's new chief of staff.

"I'm making a life change," he said, "and I would like you to hear this from me." Elliot had planned to look her up, and contact her, once he got settled in there. "As you know, I adored Brady. I admired him as a physician and as a man. Yes, he wasn't who we thought he was, but I still choose to believe he wasn't all bad." Kelsey nodded in agreement, feeling way too teary in front of a man she barely knew, but trusted. Elliot had helped her when she was desperate to get to the truth. "Kelsey, I have accepted the chief of staff position here."

"You have?" Kelsey was surprised, but happy for him, "Well congratulations, I know this hospital will thrive under your leadership, as it did Brady's. And I appreciate so much how you still respect the work Brady did here." Kelsey smiled at Elliot and he returned a smile to her. He had a sweet, round face, and his hair had grown out quite a bit more than she, again, remembered it being. He had a buzz, similar to a military man's style, when she met him. Now, it was longer and she couldn't look at it enough, she found herself imagining how it would look, outside, when the wind moved and tousled it on his head. Elliot Reiss had beautiful sandy blond hair.

The two of them talked for awhile in the hospital hallway as people rushed by en route to their destinations. They talked about Brady. They talked about her kids. They talked about taking their quest, to move on, one day at a time. Elliot also told Kelsey, when she had asked about them, that he did not move to New York with his family. His twin sons were twenty-one and in college back home, in Washington D.C., and his wife had divorced him two months ago. Kelsey tried not to pry but she did say she was *sorry* and asked what happened. And then he told her she was never truly happy in their marriage. She had stayed with him to raise the boys. *She just wasn't the woman I thought she was,* he had said, *maybe she never was.*

Before Kelsey said goodbye to Elliot, he said he hoped to see her in the hospital halls again, and she agreed. It was nice to have him there.

Chapter 21

One week later, Kelsey walked into her house following another session with Dr. Judy and she found Bailey, with worried eyes, waiting for her in the living room.

"Hi honey, everything okay?" Kelsey was setting down her purse and her laptop bag and Bailey remained silent. Kelsey walked over to her and took her hands in hers. "Tell me. You must know by now, we can get through anything."

"Those came for you today," Bailey said, pointing in the direction of the kitchen as Kelsey rounded the corner and saw a large crystal vase full of long-stemmed red roses. He had sent her one dozen roses on the twelfth day of every month since the day they were married. Two months ago they celebrated their one year anniversary, and Kelsey remembered what the card said. *Loving you will always be the greatest joy of my life. Happy 1st Anniversary! Love, Brady.* She knew the date today, the twelfth again, and all day long she had fought wanting to remember and pushed the thoughts of him, of them, out of her mind. The florist had been prepaid and instructed by Brady to deliver roses to his wife on the twelfth day of each month, indefinitely. And Kelsey had received them and loved them every time. Last month, her bouquet was delivered just days before she had uncovered Brady's lies, just days before his death. Kelsey was taken aback at this moment. It was the first bouquet she had received since he died. Since he took his own life. She wanted to grab the phone, call the florist, and say *no more!* She wanted to cancel any and all future orders that Brady may have had there, not wanting beautiful roses to ever make her feel like this again. But, she couldn't move. Bailey had followed her into the kitchen and was watching her.

She had the small card in her hand, *I will love you for the rest of forever.* She could hear him saying it, she could see him in her mind, she could feel herself in his arms. Kelsey immediately crumbled the card in her hand and let it drop to the floor. She felt the tears come on too sudden, and too fast to fight. Bailey tried to reach out to her mom, but she grabbed the flowers, vase and all, off of the table, and rushed outside to the garage. Both garage doors were wide open since she and Bailey had separately just gotten home and pulled in their vehicles. Kelsey was about to throw the entire thing into the empty trash can in the corner of the garage when she was overcome with anger.

She pulled her arm back and with extreme force, she threw the entire vase of roses against the garage wall. Glass broke and shattered everywhere and Kelsey was on her knees, sobbing. *"You son of a bitch!"* she screamed and cried in a fetal position on the garage floor and in the middle of it all, she felt someone beside her. She assumed it was Bailey until she felt unfamiliar hands gripping her shoulders as she opened her eyes and saw Elliot Reiss. He too had tears on his face. "I know, God I know, just let it out. I'm here."

Kelsey grabbed onto him as if he were pulling her from a current about to take her under. The deep waters of grief wanted to pull her under, once again, and Elliot Reiss would have done anything at that moment to save her. Moments earlier, he had parked his car on her driveway and when he got out of it, he heard the crash in the garage. And then he heard her screaming, and crying. She was in so much pain. And he understood.

They held each other for awhile, as Bailey had been crying alone in her room. She had heard the crash in the garage and knew what happened, but she never went out there. She knew her mom needed to be alone in her grief sometimes. Just as she had. She wondered if she would ever be able to think of him, hear his name, and not feel so much pain. She wished she hadn't loved him so much.

"I'm sorry, I shouldn't fall apart like this…in front of you," Kelsey said, not knowing what else to say after losing it. Elliot was still very much a stranger to her. She was in her own house, she had not expected *company*, and she at first thought his timing hadn't been perfect. But, then, she wondered if it had been. She needed to feel safe. And Elliot had provided that for her.

"It's quite alright," Elliot said, "I should have called first, but I came by to share some good news. At least, I hope you will think it's good news." Kelsey was curious as she managed to stand up, with Elliot's assistance. Glass was everywhere. What had she done? She had so much cleaning up to do now.

She left the mess and invited him to walk back inside of the house with her. In her kitchen, she told him to sit down at the table and she followed.

"I've been busy settling in at the hospital and this past week I came across the high school career program information. I know Bailey was job shadowing Brady and in the middle of an internship when…he died. If it is alright with you, I would like to invite her back to Laneview Hospital to continue and complete that training – with me."

Kelsey felt appreciative, "Thank you, I think that is a wonderful idea but that decision will be Bailey's. She's here if you would like to ask her." When Kelsey went upstairs to Bailey's bedroom, she found her trying to cover up the obvious.

She too had been crying, alone. "Hey, it's been a rough day for both of us," Kelsey pulled her close and held her, "I have some good news though, come downstairs with me. We have a guest."

After Bailey was introduced to Elliot Reiss, whom she knew had replaced Brady as the chief of staff, she sat down at the table with him. And listened. "Bailey, I have an offer for you that I sure hope you will consider," Elliot said, as Bailey looked at him directly in the eyes. He seemed familiar. He seemed kind. And his hair had taken her by surprise. In fact, when she walked into the kitchen with her mother, from the back she thought that man waiting there had looked like… her dad. Same build, and again, same sandy blond hair. "I would like you to return to your internship, pick up right where you left off, only under my direction this time. Take your time and think about it, the offer will not expire." Elliot was looking at her and she looked over at her mother. Kelsey nodded her head, as if to say, *it's okay, you should do this, for yourself,* and Bailey immediately responded, "Yes! I want to do that. I need to get back there." More than anyone knew, she needed to get back into that world. The world that had connected her to Brady Walker. She missed him, sorely, and maybe getting back into learning about medicine would somehow help her to heal a little faster.

"That's perfect, thank you for wanting to work with me. I think, very soon, we should sit down and talk about how far you've come in the program and set some new goals. Okay with you?" Elliot asked her and she smiled at him. He had a calmness, a grace, about him which she instantly liked. He was already easy to like. And she was eager to learn from him. When she heard Elliot Reiss was hired in Brady's place at Laneview Hospital, she never shared that information with her mother. She did Google his name and what she found was impressive. He was a brilliant heart specialist. One of the best in the country. A surgeon who had saved so many lives. He, like Brady, still continued to practice general medicine and perform routine surgeries, while still focusing on his specialization. That is why the hospital board at Laneview Hospital had approached him. They wanted to hire him. He was exactly what they were looking for. Bailey wanted to be that kind of doctor one day. She was impressed with Elliot Reiss.

And so was Kelsey.

After speaking to Bailey and planning for her to meet him at the hospital in just a few days, Elliot stood up from sitting at the kitchen table and asked Kelsey if he could find a garbage bag and a broom in the garage. He advised her not to back out the vehicles until he gets the glass off of the floor. "What? No. I can take care of it. I created the mess, I should be the one to clean it up," Kelsey was touched by his kindness, but she thought it wasn't necessary for him to offer.

"Then you can help me," Elliot said, smiling at her and Kelsey felt as if she had made a new friend.

***

Kelsey and Bailey were both outside on the driveway and about to separately pull their vehicles back into the garage. They now had, with Elliot's help, a glass-free garage. Just then, Miles came home after a parent of a school friend gave him a ride following basketball practice. Kelsey waved at the other mother as she pulled away from their house and Miles walked up to his mom and his sister. "What's going on?" he asked them as he glanced into the garage. That man, from a distance, had caught his eye, instantly. And, for a brief second, he thought he was seeing *his dad*. Again. Both Kelsey and Bailey saw his reaction. "Miles, come meet a friend of the family," Bailey said, leading him into the garage and Elliot met the kids halfway.

They all talked for a few minutes before Elliot said he had to get going. Before he left, he said it felt like he had a sliver of glass in his shoe, which he thought may have gotten in there when he was vacuuming the garage floor with a Shop-Vac. So he sat down on the concrete driveway and took off his left tennis shoe. And when he did, Kelsey was staring. Her kids had already gone inside of the house, so it was just her standing on the driveway, watching Elliot check the bottom of his bare foot. He had not been wearing any socks in his tennis shoes. Only one other person in her life had always done that. Kyle Newman had hated to wear socks. And apparently, Elliot Reiss preferred not to, as well.

Chapter 22

Sam Logan is now fifteen months old. When his first birthday was celebrated three months ago, he had not been mobile. He most recently learned how to pull himself up onto furniture and stand. He was now finally able to crawl, too. Sam wasn't exactly following the milestones in natural order, but he was reaching a few of them and Bree was extremely relieved and grateful.

She knew she still had a long way to go with him. But with the help of continued physical therapy, she could tell Sam is definitely on his way to learning how to walk. Three additional therapists also began seeing Sam in recent months, since he had turned one year old. There was not just a need to get him mobile, his developmental delays in all areas had prompted a developmental therapist, an occupational therapist, and a speech therapist to all get on board. Everyone was on the same page. *Let's help Sam get to where he needs to be.*

Bree was watching her son push his umbrella stroller around the kitchen, repeating the same process and the same path over and over. He could walk if he had something in front of him, to push. It was like a crutch for him, but the doctor had told Bree to allow whatever works for Sam. Just get him moving and all of that practice will eventually give him the confidence to balance independently – and walk. Pushing something, and even pulling things – like the vacuum – had a calming effect on Sam. It was one of the only times when Sam was not thinking about flapping his hands or fussing. Bree was smiling and thinking to herself, *thank God my little guy is showing some gains in this quest to become a little closer to normal,* when Kelsey knocked twice on her front door and walked in.

Kelsey knew not to say anything, at first. She is aware of how saying *hi* or *hello* in any tone of voice, especially a loud one, often alarms Sam. He couldn't handle the suddenness of *hey, I'm here* from anyone. Not even people he recognized. Jack, still, could not come home from work without alarming Sam. Bree could not even pull into the garage, with Sam in the backseat of her car, without having Sam kicking and wailing because the car had stopped and he now had to transition from the car to the house. It was just too much for him to process. All of it would seem a little crazy to an outsider, but Bree had become accustomed to Sam and *his* ways. Not that she didn't come close to dialing crazy at some point every day, but she did get it. She understood Sam, despite the fact he is nonverbal most of the time. He could say mama, dada, eat, and sleep – but that was all. The rest of his vocabulary was limited to unrecognizable jabber.

"Look at him…" Kelsey had said quietly to Bree as she sat down on the stool beside her at the island in the kitchen to watch Sam repeat his walking pattern on his tip toes, while never letting go of the stroller.

"I know… it's so nice to see him interested in doing something," Bree said, "He needs to explore and do more in order to keep learning." Kelsey nodded her head in agreement and Bree continued, "I was at the park with him yesterday, after work. Jack was working late so I thought Sam and I would enjoy the fall weather and play a little. Well, he's unsteady on the ladder to the slide so any effort it took to climb, even with me behind him, frustrated him to the point of having no interest in going down the slide. The swings get him too excited. He flaps his hands and forgets to hold on to the chains. And if someone else is swinging, forget it. I swear, if he flaps those hands any faster sometimes, he is going to fucking fly away." Bree rolled her eyes, and Kelsey giggled.

"So the park wasn't the best idea, just try again when

he's a bit bigger," Kelsey suggested and Bree disagreed. "No, it actually ended up being good for me. While Sam was sitting in the sand near the merry-go-round, and I was trying to keep him from eating it, another mom walked up. She had her son with her, I'd say he was about ten years old, and it was obvious he has Down's Syndrome. I'm sorry, but I cringe when I can take one look at a child and diagnose him or her because of how they look. It pains me. It never used to, but it does now," Bree was still struggling with the idea that Sam could one day be diagnosed and have a label. "If Sam has autism, I mean if it comes to that, at least you can't see it at first glance. I know that sounds awful, but that's the way I feel. I don't want people to be able to see special needs written all over my son."

"It's okay, Bree," Kelsey reassured her, "You have accepted so much in the past year and a half. So many moms would not be as far as you are right now, in terms of getting Sam the help he needs. You are my hero, sweets. I admire you for what you do every day for your little guy." Kelsey squeezed Bree's hand on the countertop.

"Everyone has something, I'm just doing the best I can to deal with mine," Bree said, sighing, "So how are things? Are the kids okay? Are you surviving?"

"We are all doing fine," Kelsey replied, "but it's there. It's always there. Thinking about it, thinking about Brady, no longer brings tears to my eyes – but it still stings, and I think it always will."

"I understand. In a way I do know, somewhat, how you feel," Bree said, still keeping an eye on Sam, and then looking at

Kelsey. "I hated Nic for a long time, and even though I'm past those awful feelings I had directed at him for so long, it does still sting. And I *know* it always will."

Kelsey was trying to move forward. Seeing her children flourish, comforted her. Miles was working harder to get better grades in school so he could remain on the basketball team and join a traveling team next spring. Kelsey made him promise to study hard, ask for help in any subject if he needs it, and then she would agree to allow him to add more basketball to his young life. Bailey was thriving in school, in sports, and with her internship at the hospital. She had been working alongside Dr. Elliot Reiss for six weeks now. Bailey continued to tell Kelsey how much she is learning, and she liked to say, *"It's no wonder Elliot is a heart specialist because he has the biggest heart of anyone I've ever met."* Kelsey agreed. That man was a godsend to her daughter. And Elliot had so easily become a dear friend to Kelsey as well. He called her at least once a week to report on how *terrific* Bailey is working as an intern at Laneview. She welcomed those phone calls, and often looked forward to them. And she told Bree just as much.

"So what's his story? He's divorced right?" Bree asked, rather directly, and Kelsey knew what she was implying.

"He is divorced, and I know what you're getting at, so I'm just going to tell you he is a friend to me. That is all. He and I just happened to find some common ground. We both were burned by Brady, and we both still love and miss him. He gets it, and that bonds us. There is nothing sexual between us. He is becoming more like a brother to me than anything else." Kelsey was speaking honestly, and Bree just smiled at her.

"Some of the best relationships begin as friendships," Bree said, smirking, "So what does he look like?" Bailey had said it first to Kelsey during dinner one evening, and Miles agreed. Elliot Reiss and Kyle Newman shared some similar features and the same great hair. Kelsey had told her children, she too, noticed this. She also told them how Elliot does not wear socks, which made all three of them laugh. Kyle owned socks but never wore them. There were still several pairs of unworn socks upstairs in a dresser drawer that had belonged to Kyle. And then Kelsey told her kids exactly how she felt about recognizing those things in Elliot in the past few months. *"I think, when we see your dad in Elliot or when he says or does something to remind us of him, we should take that as a sign your dad is with us. We know he's here, watching us, guiding us, and loving us. It's such a blessing to have Elliot as our friend now."* And Kelsey also shared all of that with Bree, who didn't say anything more to Kelsey regarding Elliot. She was just going to sit back and watch this love story in the making. Bree could see it was already unfolding, but she also knew it was too soon for Kelsey to recognize or welcome it.

***

As Kelsey walked away from Bree's house and back across the street, she saw a familiar car on the driveway. It was a silver Lexus with the license plates ER MD 1. She smiled to herself. Elliot Reiss. Medical Doctor. And as for the number one, yes, he was a top doctor in New York City. A heart specialist who had, slowly, managed to begin mending her heart. She harbored no romantic feelings for him, she just felt comfortable and safe in his presence. Even just hearing his voice on the phone always brought a sense of peace over her.

She walked into the living room to find a Lego tower, built high, beginning on her coffee table and reaching up to her chin when she took a closer look at it. Miles and Elliot, who were both on their knees on the carpet in front of the table, told her simultaneously to *back away, before it falls!* Kelsey giggled, and did as they asked as she sat down on the couch behind them. It was not like Elliot to just stop by the house, but it was a nice surprise. He sensed what she was thinking, so he spoke first. "I hope you don't mind my impromptu visit, I was hoping to catch Bailey to discuss next week's schedule at the hospital. I got the board's permission to allow Bailey in the operating room for a bypass surgery, and I wanted to tell her in person," Elliot explained.

"Oh my goodness, you know she is going to be thrilled!" Kelsey said, clapping her hands together, "but she's not here right now. You can hang out if you want, until she gets home." Miles cheered at his mom's suggestion and Elliot said he would *love to*. The two of them continued with their Lego project and Kelsey went into the kitchen to see what she could whip up for dinner. And then she wondered if Elliot would want to stay and eat with them.

The four of them ended up ordering out for pizza while talking and laughing and just enjoying each other's company throughout the evening. Kelsey had been right, Bailey was absolutely thrilled at the idea of observing her first surgery. She was beginning to veer away from the aspect of studying to become a pediatrician. She now wanted to be a surgeon of some sort. Exactly what area of expertise, she did not know yet. Brady had taught her so much about the brain, and now Elliot was teaching her all about the heart. She agreed with her mother, Elliot had become a friend of the family, and for so many reasons she hoped he would stick around for a very long time.

Charlie stopped in after football practice so he and Bailey were catching up in the kitchen while he ate some leftover pizza, and Miles was upstairs taking a shower. It was a school night, and Kelsey was adamant about him being in bed by nine o'clock. He was not a star student and he needed his rest in order to concentrate and get through the school day.

Kelsey saw the Lego tower was still on her coffee table as she sat down on the couch and handed Elliot a glass of wine, and then she took a sip of hers. "Thank you for making both of my kids happy campers tonight. One is easily pleased building Legos and the other is looking forward to the idea of watching you saw open a human being's chest and work your miracles on a beating heart." Elliot was laughing out loud at Kelsey's description and she took another sip of her wine when he spoke to her. "You do not have to thank me when your kids, and you, make me just as happy," Elliot didn't know if he should go there, yet. He had fallen for her, heart first, but he knew she had so much more healing left to do. She didn't seem interested in beginning another relationship yet, and he was content with simply being her friend. "I mean that, your friendship has come to mean so much to me," Elliot continued speaking to her, "Here I am, new to this city, having left my family and friends behind in D.C., and you've made me feel like this could be home to me someday. I mean, this city," he added, carefully correcting himself, and Kelsey smiled at him, knowing he also had meant her and her kids.

"I feel the same way, Elliot," Kelsey replied, finishing off the wine in her glass, "Your friendship has seen me through some rough moments, and having you in our lives feels nice." They weren't sitting close, but he had started to move toward her when Miles came barreling down the stairs. He had wet hair, bare feet, and he was wearing his bedtime attire – a white t-shirt and pajama pants. "I need to clean up my Legos for tonight, Elliot will you help me?" The two of them dismantled their masterpiece and put all of the pieces into the container, which had been sitting empty all evening on the floor in the living room.

After Miles told them both good night, he headed back upstairs. And then Elliot said he had to get going, back to his apartment in the city, near the hospital. As he reached into the front pocket of his tight-fitting jeans, he pulled out his keys but lost hold of them and dropped them on the carpet in front of him. Kelsey had been standing near him so she bent down to pick them up, just as Elliot had. And that is when their hands touched. "Oh, sorry," she said attempting to pull her hand away, but before she did Elliot made an intentional effort to softly touch her hand with his and held it for a moment as he smiled at her. And when he told her goodnight, and walked out of her home, she was left standing there, still feeling the surge of electricity that had shot through her body. And she heard her own words, to Bree just hours earlier, *There is nothing sexual between us. He is becoming more like a brother to me than anything else.* And then she thought, to herself, *I might have to recant those words... considering I can now see myself wanting to take off that man's clothes.*

Chapter 23

Kelsey continued to fight her feelings, and she told Dr. Judy as much during a session. She didn't want to allow another man into her heart, in fear that it would just get broken again. No matter how wonderful a feeling it was for her to have Elliot in her life, in her children's lives, she just couldn't allow herself to love again. Not this soon. It had only been six months since Brady's death.

It was early spring, everything around her was beginning to show new life, the trees, the flowers, and she had admitted, in therapy, how she felt different. She felt a little bit alive again.

Elliot had spent the holidays with them, because he had nowhere else to go. His sons had chosen to stay in D.C. with their mother, and Kelsey had invited him to spend the time celebrating with her, her kids, and Bree's family. Elliot fit nicely and comfortably into their mix, and he had faith that, one day, Kelsey would be ready to share a life with him. No matter how much time she needed, he believed Kelsey is every bit worth the wait.

"So you are putting yourself on a time schedule of some sort now?" Dr. Judy asked Kelsey, "Do you see a reason for not allowing yourself, *at this time*, to fall in love again? Like, maybe, you're afraid of getting hurt, of suffering loss, or not being able to handle any more pain that is often times so much a part of life?"

Kelsey nodded her head, "Yes, all of the above," she said, "With Kyle, life had been so easy. We just fell into a comfortable and happy life together. With Brady, it was exciting and electric. The intensity of seizing every moment was sometimes overwhelming. And now, with Elliot, he just fits. He fits like a surgical glove. Tight, secure, and so perfectly molded to the hands. I feel, with Elliot, the same kind of instant comfort in our relationship that I experienced with Kyle, and now I have been feeling some of that electricity like I had found with Brady. Elliot is a mix of the two great loves I've had in my life. Is that a perfect concoction, or a recipe for disaster?"

Dr. Judy laughed. Kelsey certainly had a way with words sometimes. It's no wonder she is a writer. "I think, no matter what, it's worth pursuing," Dr. Judy advised, "We have decisions to make in our lives, and at the very same time we also must leave so much up to chance. But, sometimes, if we don't take those chances we can be sure to one day find ourselves looking back. When that happens do you want to say *I can't believe I did that?* Or, do you want to say, *I wish I had done that!* It's your life, it's your heart. But, just remember, the third time is a charm."

***

It was time for Kelsey to make a change. Spring is a time for new beginnings. Kelsey's kids were beyond excited when she sat them down in their living room and told them they were getting an in-ground swimming pool. She and Kyle had talked about it for years, but never did it. It was something Kelsey had always wanted, and now as her children were getting older, she felt good about both of them being fantastic swimmers and her house could be a place where their friends could gather.

She was showing them the plans she had drawn up by the owner of a popular pool store in downtown Greenville. It was not a nationwide chain, it was just a family-owned swimming pool business. A crew installed pools and took care of any maintenance. Kelsey knew she would need help with the maintenance, not having a man in the house, so she hired Aquarius Pools to dig a gigantic hole in her backyard and make it look like a vacation spot.

As she was showing her kids the brochure from the pool store, and had given them the task of picking out the color and pattern of the swimming pool liner, Elliot arrived.

The kids immediately shared the *awesome* news with him and he seemed just as excited. He proceeded to tell Kelsey that he knew of someone who excelled in landscaping. The guy had recently moved to New York, from out of state, from a previously owned beautiful home with exquisite landscaping and a flower garden. That same guy was now living in an apartment in the city with not even a lawn to take care of. Kelsey was smiling, her eyes sparkling, by the time Elliot finished his *personal* story.

"Tell your friend, he's hired," she said laughing and Elliot pumped both of his fists in the air, saying, "Yes!" Then, he suggested, *maybe, this weekend they could get together and talk about ideas…did she want rose bushes, or wild flowers mixed with green and purple bushes? It was, of course completely up to her, and he was ready for the job.* Kelsey was happy seeing how she had just made her kids – and Elliot – ready and looking forward to something new. Something fun.

Kelsey had been thinking, constantly, about telling Elliot how she might be ready to explore their feelings for each other. Maybe take their relationship to the next level? She sometimes, especially lately, had been daydreaming about what it might feel like to have him kiss her. Her thoughts were interrupted amid all of their chatter as Elliot's cell phone beeped. It was the hospital and he had an emergency surgery to perform. As he rushed out of the house, he looked back at Kelsey and said *I'll call you later. Can't wait to be your landscaper.* And she smiled at him, telling him to *be careful driving…and good luck with that surgery.*

Less than five minutes later, Bree was calling Kelsey's cell phone. "Hello sweets," Kelsey answered, feeling good about her life again and still feeling high from the evening's excitement. "Kel!" There was panic in Bree's voice, "Here we fucking go again! Jack and I are at Laneview, the pediatrician found Sam has a heart problem. He needs surgery tonight, please get here. Be with me. I can't lose another son," Bree was crying and Kelsey felt herself beginning to unravel. *Not again. Please God, not again.*

Chapter 24

Kelsey brought both Bailey and Miles along with her to the hospital. They were scared for Sam's life, too. While driving en route to the hospital Bailey said to Kelsey, "You know that was Elliot's emergency, don't you? He is the heart surgeon who will be taking care of Sam's little heart tonight. Mom, I've seen Elliot in action, and even though I do not know what in the world is happening with Sam, what kind of heart condition he could possibly have, I know Elliot can fix him." At that moment, Kelsey felt hopeful…and she was going to hold on to that hope with everything she had.

When she, once again, rushed through the emergency doors at Laneview Hospital, this time with her children in tow, they found Bree and Jack in the surgical waiting room. Bree was crying again and Jack had his arms around her, looking just as forlorn.

"Tell us what happened," Kelsey said, as they all sat down and listened to Bree explain what is now going on with Sam.

"Sam had his eighteen-month checkup with the pediatrician this afternoon and she was talking about diagnosing him with autism. I've seen this coming, Kel, I think we all have, so I was prepared and in agreement. Dr. Michelle proceeded with his checkup and stalled when she listened to his heart. She kept going back for another listen. She was alarmed. She wanted immediate blood drawn from him and she put a rush on the results. She told me a diagnosis like autism can sometimes stem from a genetic disorder. I told her Sam is a healthy boy, and then she told me she didn't like what she was hearing today when she pressed her stethoscope to his chest. She knew just what she was looking for when she put a rush on the blood work. She later diagnosed Sam with Williams Syndrome." Kelsey had never heard of it, and Bree began to tell her what she had just learned about it today. Williams Syndrome is a genetic condition characterized by medical problems, including cardiovascular disease, developmental delays, and learning disabilities. Jack explained how Dr. Michelle found a problem with one of Sam's blood vessels, a narrowing in his aorta. The aorta is the largest artery in the human body which originates from the left ventricle of the heart. Its job is to distribute oxygenated blood to all parts of the body. "And Sam's aorta was in a serious enough degree of narrowing to prompt emergency surgery to correct the defect," Bree said, trying to hold herself together, "Dr. Michelle said the degrees can range from trivial to severe, and Elliot told us, right before surgery, that this process, if caught in time, will allow Sam to live a long life with periodic cardiac monitoring."

"Elliot is the best heart doctor in this hospital, and one of the top in this country!" Bailey interrupted, "Sam is in very good hands." Bree reached for Bailey and pulled her close, whispering, "Thank you, honey, I sure hope so."

***

Three hours later, Miles was asleep, curled up on two chairs. Kelsey had already decided her kids were not going to school tomorrow. It had turned out to be a long, worrisome night for all of them.

They were sitting in silence when the door opened and Elliot walked in. His scrubs were damp from sweat, around the neckline, and his sandy blond hair was matted and sticking out of his surgical cap on his forehead and around his ears. And then Kelsey saw how his eyes looked hopeful and his smile was wide. *Oh thank God!* All four of them immediately stood up as Elliot said, "Sam is a champ. He is going to be just fine. The surgery was a success. He had a moderate to somewhat severe degree of narrowing in his aorta, thank goodness Dr. Zahn listened to him today and caught that. She saved his life."

"And so did you!" Bree exclaimed as she threw her arms around his neck and Kelsey stood there with tears welling up in her eyes. *What a wonderful man.*

"I'm happy to put that smile on your face, Bree, and the relief in your eyes," Elliot said as Jack shook his hand, firm and swiftly, and so full of gratitude. "You can see him now, he's still in recovery, but go on down there, third door on the left."

As Jack and Bree quickly left the waiting room, Bailey spoke to Elliot first. "I knew you could do it, I told them you are the best heart surgeon ever, and I will always believe that is true." Bailey hugged Elliot's neck and this time he was the one with tears in his eyes. "Thanks, kiddo. That means the world to me."

When Bailey left to go buy a couple bottles of water for her and her mom, Kelsey and Elliot were left alone with a sleeping Miles. "Who knew when I rushed out of your house tonight, I would be doing my best to save your dear friend's baby?" Elliot stated, feeling relief, the same relief he felt each time he saved a life in the operating room. This time, however, it felt a little different for him. It was personal.

"Oh my, how we've had our share of panic and heartbreak, but tonight changed my outlook on happy endings," Kelsey said to him, "I mean it, Elliot, I will be forever grateful to you for what you did for Sam, and for Bree and Jack."

"I want you to believe in happy endings," Elliot said moving closer to her, "I want to be a part of *your* happy ending. You may not be ready for me, or for us, anytime soon but when you are, I will be right here, waiting." As he finished saying those words to her, she pressed her lips against his. He responded with a tenderness that quickly escalated to an aggressive seal between them, their lips touching, tongues intertwining. Their desire was mounting as they regretfully pulled themselves away from each other, in fear of Miles waking up or Bailey returning.

"You're an amazing woman, Kelsey," Elliot said, trying to control his urge to drag her into the first supply closet they could find and make passionate love to her. He smiled at the thought, and she was thinking much of the same as she pondered, *what is it with me and first kisses in this hospital?* "It's been a long time and if I didn't have two kids with me tonight, I would de-scrub you, Dr. Reiss." They both laughed out loud in unison, and individually imagined what their first time would be like. And they each hoped to find out very soon.

Chapter 25

Two weeks had gone by with Sam's recovery going exceptionally well. Bree and Jack both felt reassured that Sam is going to be fine, but they knew the signs to look for if that main blood vessel were to ever begin narrowing again. Patients can suffer from chest pain or tightness, fatigue after increased activity, or heart palpitations. Sam being able to communicate those symptoms would be an altogether different story.

Any eighteen-month-old could have difficulty communicating their chest hurts, but this is Sam who doesn't talk at all. Bree needed to know how else or what else to look for if her son begins having heart trouble again. She would go to the extreme and visit the doctor every day, if she had to, to have her listen through her stethoscope for an abnormal heart sound, which Bree just learned is the definition of a heart murmur. But, an easier and saner way, she was told, would be to watch and listen for shortness of breath in Sam, and also be aware if he wears out more quickly than usual after playing or simply moving around.

Bree had most definitely gotten a miracle when her son's heart condition was detected in time to save his life. While Sam was in surgery, she sat in silence with her wonderful, supportive husband by her side, and she had prayed. She prayed to a God she had been turning to more than ever since Sam was born. Her faith was tested when she lost her thirteen-year-old son and it was renewed and strengthened when she was blessed with another son. Sam had changed her life. Changed her. She was now more patient, more compassionate, and more understanding with everyone – especially those with special needs. God had given her Sam because she could handle him. Bree believed that now. And she realized that while praying the night Dr. Elliot Reiss was repairing her baby boy's heart in the operating room at Laneview Hospital. *Please God, whatever lies ahead, I know I can handle it, just please let Sam live. If he lives with a syndrome or with autism, I've got this. Please give him back to me.* That prayer alone gave Bree a strength she had never known before. Her son had, in the eighteen months of his life, brought her a stress and a worry she now lived with all of the time. But, he had also brought her and Jack, and all of those who knew and loved him, so much joy. Some days, she certainly did not know what she was going to do with him. But those were also the same days, and the same moments, when she always reminded herself of how she also did not know what she would ever do without him.

***

Construction for the in-ground swimming pool was complete at Kelsey's house, and the landscaping development was in full swing. Kelsey was relaxing, poolside, in a lounge chair, in the already-hot May sun while she watched Miles jump into the deep end, splashing both his sister and Charlie who were floating on rafts very near where he purposely chose to jump in. Through her sunglasses, Kelsey moved her eyes over to the landscaper. Elliot was wearing khaki cargo shorts, ankle-high work boots probably with no socks, and no shirt. Kelsey couldn't take her eyes off of his already tanned skin. She watched how his back and shoulder muscles moved as he worked in the dirt, planting shrubs and flowers. He was working entirely too hard, but had obviously been enjoying himself. She knew how much he missed being able to tend to his yard like when he owned a home. Just as she was thinking about slipping into her flip flops, sitting on the concrete beside her lounge chair, and walking through the grass in the yard to see him, to talk to him, to maybe touch him on his arm, or on his face, Kelsey's thoughts were interrupted."Hi, mom!" Charlie was looking toward the open gate on the side of the house and Blair Thompson was walking through it.

She was wearing a purple tankini swim top and matching scrunch short bottoms with a sheer cover-up over top of it all. It had been almost twenty years since Kelsey had seen her, and this woman was still striking – even in her sixties. Kelsey was wearing a solid black bikini top and matching bikini bottoms and at the moment she wished she had her own cover-up on, but she was so excited to see her that she leapt out of her chair, slipped on her sandals and met that woman in her yard. "You have got to be kidding me, welcome to my home, finally! You are as lovely as ever," Kelsey said responding to Blair's open arms as she hugged her close and Blair said, "Oh honey, you are the beautiful one, so much younger than me." The two women laughed and Charlie was smiling at them both, from the swimming pool. He had told his mom, repeatedly, how Kelsey Walker said she is always welcome at her home, anytime. Today, Blair Thompson decided it was time.

***

Kelsey offered Blair an iced tea as they sat underneath the glass-topped charcoal wrought-iron umbrella table on the patio. Blair had said she tries to avoid basking in the direct sunlight at her age. It was obvious she had taken exceptional care of her skin, all of her life. "Can you believe this? After all of these years, our children found a friendship, a bond that keeps getting stronger, if you ask me," Kelsey stated, looking at Blair Thompson, still in disbelief that she was even there.

"I can believe it," Blair said, "because I've lived long enough to know that life is full of surprises, good and bad." Blair was speaking from experience, for sure. She was speaking to Kelsey because she knew she also had not sailed through life unaffected by heartache and grief. Too many times. Blair was feeling a little ashamed for her earlier actions. Kelsey had not known, but Blair had tried to keep her son away from *those people,* after she had found out Brady Walker was a murderer who had committed suicide to avoid punishment for his crimes. Charlie fought her demand and said he would never abide by what she forbade him to do. He loved Bailey and her family and he wanted to be there for them, through it all. He then told her that it was, in fact, him who first doubted Brady Walker was the person they all believed him to be. He told his mother the complete details of the phone conversation he overheard and how everything unraveled from there. If he had not told Kelsey the truth, more people could have been harmed at Brady's hand. That man was spiraling out of control, trying to protect his wife and family from the truth. He knew what the ramifications would be, so he became desperate, which led to his downfall. Charlie had taught Blair – the woman who gave him a home and a good life and unconditional love – much more than she could ever have taught him. From the moment he was born, he was an unbelievable blessing to her. He had changed her life, fulfilled her dream to become a mother. And now, two decades later, Charlie had exemplified to Blair how protecting the people you love is more important than anything else.

"You couldn't be more right about that," Kelsey wholeheartedly agreed with Blair, "I'm in a good place now in my life, as are my kids, but there were times I did not know how much more we could handle."

"I used to read a book, Winnie the Pooh, in fact, to Charlie when he was a little boy," Blair started to explain, "and there was a quote in there by the author, A.A. Mine, and it goes like this, *"Promise me you'll always remember…You're braver than you believe, and stronger than you seem, and smarter than you think."* Kelsey was smiling at the woman sitting beside her. Such an inspiration. First, twenty years ago, for Kelsey, and now again. "Thank you for sharing that with me, I will carry those words with me and remember them when I need to most."

"I need you to do something for me, Kelsey," Blair said, suddenly sounding too serious and Kelsey responded, "I will certainly try to," and listened.

And that is when Blair Thompson told Kelsey, she is dying. "I have an incurable blood disease. I was diagnosed with multiple myeloma, which is a cancer affecting the blood cells in my bone marrow. Doctors use certain criteria to classify myeloma on a scale from one to three. I have three, the most advanced." Tears were seeping out from beneath Kelsey's sunglasses. *No, it couldn't be true. Not this woman, this pillar of strength. She couldn't give up without a fight. What about Charlie? She was all he had. And then she retracted her own thought, Charlie is a part of her family and always will be.* And then she understood exactly why Blair Thompson came to her home today.

"Blair, you have to fight this!" Kelsey said, adamantly, "Get the treatments, fight to survive. You can do this. Listen to me, you can beat this dreadful disease, people do it all of the time!" Kelsey felt as if she was begging her not to give up, not to give in.

"I hear you, but the odds are sadly against me as the doctors are telling me my kidneys will soon fail. The cancer is too far along, my organs are too weak to handle chemotherapy," Blair explained, wiping away the tears on her own face, "I have to tell Charlie tonight. But, Kelsey, I wanted to talk to you first. I need to be reassured my son will have a home to come to when he needs to feel loved. I know he already feels welcome and so very loved by you and your family. Financially, I am leaving my son well taken care of. He can live in our penthouse, or anywhere he would like – but a house is not a home without those you love."

"My home will always be open to Charlie. I don't want to think about you leaving him, but I will give you the peace of mind that you need. My home with my children will always be Charlie's home, too. He can live with us if it comes to that. Please know if… the time comes…" Kelsey could hardly say those words, "I will get him through his grief the best I know how. I am not you, though, and I never will be." Kelsey was crying now and Blair Thompson was shedding on her own tears when she pulled her close and whispered, "Thank you from the very bottom of my heart, a heart that feels like it is breaking right now. My son is going to need you more than ever."

Chapter 26

After a full day in the sun, and in the shade, Charlie and his mom left to go home. Kelsey felt overwhelmed with sadness watching Blair Thompson walk away with her son, knowing what she was about to tell him tonight, once they were back home at their penthouse in the city.

The kids were showered and in bed at eleven-thirty, the swimming and the sun had worn out everyone. Elliot was sitting outside in a chair near the pool, it was dark but the pool lights were glowing on his face as Kelsey sat down beside him. "I would go inside and hang out with you, but I'm a dirty, sweaty mess from being your yard slave today," Elliot teased her and Kelsey took his hand in hers. "Yeah, your fingers do look a little grubby, doctor. You better go inside and take a shower before you touch me with them."

Elliot looked at her, really bore his eyes into hers, and he quietly asked her if she was *ready*, and she replied, "More than you know," with a sexiness in her voice that sent sensations through his entire body. He followed her inside and she led him upstairs to her master bedroom. She gave him a fresh fluffy white towel and a matching wash cloth while she stood in the bathroom, off of her bedroom, with him. She didn't want to, but she left, to give him his privacy.

Ten minutes later, pacing in her bedroom, still wearing her bikini, Kelsey could hear the shower water continue to run. She didn't dwell on what she was about to do. She just opened the bathroom door, noticing the steam in the air which had fogged the mirror on the wall above the sink and vanity, and she closed the door and locked it behind her. She opened the shower door just as Elliot was rinsing the shampoo from his hair. When he opened his eyes, he saw her standing there. Neither one of them spoke as Kelsey reached behind her back with both of her hands and undid the clasp on her bikini top, and then she slipped off her bikini bottoms. Elliot was staring at her body as she was his. She saw a fit, beautiful man, and his manhood had taken her by surprise. He was, as they say, *well-endowed*. Maybe her psychiatrist was right, *the third time would be a charm.*

As she stepped into the shower with him, he pulled her into a passionate kiss. The water was falling onto both of their faces as they found themselves lost in each other, and hungry for more. Elliot touched her breasts with his fingers first and then found them with his mouth. He worked his way down her body, kneeling before her in the shower. She too touched him in places, with her fingers and with her mouth, which drove him completely crazy. The vent in the bathroom was still running as they shut off the shower water and kept moving their hands over each other's bodies. They were dripping wet when they made their way out of the shower and Kelsey threw a towel down onto the floor for them to step onto. She wanted to take him into her bed, but neither one of them could wait any longer. It was happening on the marble tiled floor in the bathroom. Elliot pulled her close and kissed her full on the mouth. She responded with a desire she had not felt in such a long time. His hands were on her, his fingers were inside her, she touched him, she took him into her mouth, and the pattern continued, repeated, until he was inside of her and neither one of them could stop what was happening. They had already fallen in love, months ago, and now, finally, they had become lovers.

Afterward, Kelsey led him into her bed, asking him to spend the night with her. They made love again and, later, when Elliot had fallen asleep, Kelsey laid in his arms, with her head on his chest. She could hear his heart beating. This man. This heart doctor. Had won her heart. She loved him.

She was awake most of the night, thinking about her life and all that has happened to her. It hasn't been easy, but *no one* has it easy. She thought of Blair Thompson and prayed for her to be able to continue her life with Charlie for many more years to come. She thought of Bree, with Jack and Sam. They had many challenges and hurdles ahead, but who didn't? Then she thought of her children. They are her world, and she knew how incredibly blessed she is to have them both. And now there's Elliot. A man who had, without a doubt, given her another chance in her life to love and be loved. *My goodness*, she thought, as she finally started to fall asleep in her bed with this amazing man beside her, *I feel as if the seams of my life have been let out a bit.*

About the Author

There is something wrong with that child. We have all heard those words before. Most of us have said them. Or at least thought them. But, none of us ever think we are going to be the one with a child who has special needs. At least I never imagined it being me.

Eleven years ago, my first child was born. A baby girl I wanted to name Bailey before she was even conceived. Boy or girl, I wanted a child named Bailey. From babyhood on, she has been a joy. So easy. She reached every milestone early. Raising her was like dealing with an adult in a little body. She understood. She learned. She listened. She played. She was, as a baby, and still is today, an old soul. She has always known things beyond her years of experience. She makes parenting easy. When Bailey was twenty-six months old, her brother Connor was born. I remember telling my husband, Mike prior to us getting pregnant with our second child that I was ready to tackle having two kids. I was ready for a challenge. And what a *challenge* that would be.

Connor was born (almost) nine years ago, and he literally came out of the birth canal mad at the world. Instantly, he just could not get settled outside of the comfort and quiet of the womb. I remember one of the OB nurses in the hospital room, who was trying to get Baby Connor settled on the scale to weigh him right after his birth, saying, "He is grunting over here like a little old man." So fussy.

It wasn't until Connor turned five months old that I began to question his development. He wouldn't sit up. If we propped him up into a sitting position, Connor would stiffen his body and throw himself back onto the floor. He wanted to be flat on his back. If we placed him on his tummy, he would fight to roll over onto his back. After nearly five months of physical therapy, Connor sat up independently for the first time! He did this on his first birthday. I realized that most one-year-olds are full-blown crawling, or even walking by then. But that was okay with me, because Connor made it. He attained a goal.

Goals. Lots of them. Sitting up independently was just the first of so many goals that doctors and therapists and teachers – and his mommy and daddy – have set for Connor. Seeing Connor attain any goal, no matter how small, is relief, satisfaction, gratitude, and pride all wrapped up into one.

My son was diagnosed with mild to moderate autism when he was four years old. He's not high-functioning, not yet verbal enough, not yet academically ready for school work, but he has made some significant gains through the years. I've never stopped wanting more and expecting more for my son. So many goals have yet to be attained and I will continue hoping and praying that one day I can check another goal off of his list.

Throughout Seams and Unraveled, I have emphasized, repeatedly, how everyone has *something* in this life. No one gets by unscathed. All of you, those who know me and those who have read my books, must realize by now that I believe challenges, hurt, and heartache can all be overcome. Eventually. It's just a matter of putting one foot in front of the other, one day at a time.

Thank you for reading!

love,

Lori Bell